"We still have to settle our bet," Gavin reminded her.

"What do you mean?" Stacy asked warily.

"The completion of my being vamped. Tonight I just want to enjoy being with a beautiful woman. Couldn't we just be the vamp*er* and the vamp*ee*?"

"Beautiful woman?" Stacy's voice was incredulous. Gavin suspected she'd been called many things in her life, but beautiful wasn't one of them. Overhead, a sleek silver-dollar moon followed along as they drove. It was a night for lovers, or, if he were a horror fan, he might say for creatures on the prowl. Stacy hadn't responded to his teasing quip about the vamping. Maybe he'd approach her from another direction. He smiled and touched Stacy's shoulder.

"Do you feel it?"

"What?"

"The power of the night, when the creatures of darkness come to life." He caught her attention and watched her face light up as she turned to face him.

"Look, Stacy, look at the moon. I want you to know I'm prepared to be vamped. Do your best . . . or your worst," he suggested with a grin.

She looked nervous—and tempted. "I don't know what you expect me to do," she said softly.

"I seem to recall several definitions of vamping in the dictionary. If you don't want to seduce me, well—how would you feel about coming over here and biting my neck?"

WHAT ARE *LOVESWEPT* ROMANCES?

They are stories of true romance and touching emotion. We believe those two very important ingredients are constants in our highly sensual and very believable stories in the *LOVESWEPT* line. Our goal is to give you, the reader, stories of consistently high quality that may sometimes make you laugh, sometimes make you cry, but are always fresh and creative and contain many delightful surprises within their pages.

Most romance fans read an enormous number of books. Those they truly love, they keep. Others may be traded with friends and soon forgotten. We hope that each *LOVESWEPT* romance will be a treasure—a "keeper." We will always try to publish

LOVE STORIES YOU'LL NEVER FORGET
BY AUTHORS YOU'LL ALWAYS REMEMBER

The Editors

Loveswept 546

Sandra Chastain
Lean Mean
Loving Machine

BANTAM BOOKS
NEW YORK · TORONTO · LONDON · SYDNEY · AUCKLAND

LEAN MEAN LOVING MACHINE
A Bantam Book / June 1992

If you would be interested in receiving protective vinyl
covers for your Loveswept books, please write to this address
for information:

Loveswept
Bantam Books
P.O. Box 985
Hicksville, NY 11802

ISBN 0-553-44136-1

Published simultaneously in the United States and Canada

Bantam Books are published by Bantam Books, a division of
Bantam Doubleday Dell Publishing Group, Inc. Its trademark,
consisting of the words "Bantam Books" and the portrayal of
a rooster, is Registered in U.S. Patent and Trademark Office
and in other countries. Marca Registrada. Bantam Books, 666
Fifth Avenue, New York, New York 10103.

PRINTED IN THE UNITED STATES OF AMERICA

OPM   0 9 8 7 6 5 4 3 2 1

This one's for you, Karen,
because you're special.

One

"Two dollars says he gets a hit."

Stacy Lanham propped her feet on a soft-drink crate and leaned back to watch the Atlanta Braves play the Dodgers.

"You're on, girl." Lonnie Short dragged up a stool and sat down, pulling a grease-stained cloth from his coveralls and wiping his bald head.

The pinch hitter stood in, shifting his feet as the pitcher went into his delivery. One pitch, and the ball careened through the diving infielders as if it had eyes.

As the batter pulled up on third, Stacy turned and held out her hand. "Pay up, Lonnie."

Lonnie shook his head and unfolded a crumpled mass of bills, peeling out two and handing them to the grinning girl.

"If you'd been playing shortstop, the ball wouldn't have gotten through and I'd still have my money, not to mention the ownership of this garage, which your father promised to sell me on his deathbed."

"Now, Lonnie, you know that Daddy didn't promise you any such thing, and the Braves don't draft women."

"Well, you'd be a lot more use to them than you are to me," he grumbled as he came to his feet and moseyed out of the small office that adjoined the empty work bays.

Stacy stood. "Let's go home. The dispatcher'll call if there's trouble. I want to watch the game in color."

"You just don't want to take a chance on me winning that two dollars back, Stacy."

"Poo! You know I'll win." Stacy followed him, ready to continue the argument that had become an ongoing pastime in the last year. "Besides, grumpy, I'm almost as good a mechanic as you are, and I drive these trucks a whole lot better."

"Fine," Lonnie agreed, "then drive one of them out to Vegas and see if you can pick up some money to pay some of our bills. At least you'd have to put on a dress in a casino. Just look at you. Grease on your face and under your fingernails, your hair going every way but Sunday. A girl like you ought to be out having fun, finding a man and getting married."

Lonnie the Matchmaker was at work again. "A minute ago you thought I ought to be playing shortstop for the Braves. Besides, I'm not a serious gambler."

"I don't understand why not. You always win, which is more than your daddy could say."

"You know I have a ten-dollar limit, and I never gamble on anything that matters. If I did, I'd lose—just like Daddy did."

"How would you know? You've never tried."

"That's right, and I'm not going to. I saw Lucky

take a fortune and gamble it away. It killed my mother and turned us into grease monkeys."

"At least in Vegas you might meet one of those millionaires, for all the good that would do. You don't know diddley about vamping a man."

"I know all I need to know," she protested. "I just don't want to. I like my life the way it is, safe and sane."

"And dull. I'll bet you if an interested man walked through the door, you wouldn't have the wildest idea of how to catch his attention."

"And you'd be wrong."

"Anastasia Lanham, you're chicken. I'll make you a wager you can't refuse. You vamp the next man who comes into the shop. If you fail, you'll clean out the grease pit. If you win, I'll clean it, and you can forget my week's pay."

Stacy grinned at her oldest and dearest friend. She knew he worried about her. Running a trucking garage wasn't normally a woman's job. It hadn't been her father's either, as he'd quickly discovered. Lucky Lanham had been a baseball player whose knees had gone bad. During his winning years, he'd bought up small moving companies and garages with the idea that after he retired he could be his own boss.

Nobody but she and Lonnie knew about her father's later addiction to gambling, or how his coast-to-coast fleet of semis and garages had dwindled down to one. And nobody had believed that she'd take over running the garage when her father had died six years earlier. But it had been something he'd always expected she'd do. What he could never have expected was that she would become the natural gambler that he'd never been. Lucky had always lost. Stacy never did.

Stacy had been worried all day about where Lonnie's pay would come from this week. Every mail brought more bills and fewer checks. She couldn't really withhold his pay, but the bet might give her a few days' grace period. Besides, she knew every eligible man in the county.

More in fun than anything else, Stacy began planning her strategy. She wasn't above a little bet rigging, if it would stop Lonnie's matchmaking. "Your check and the grease pit, if I succeed?"

"That's right."

"Agreed."

"Ah, sweet justice. I'm about to be a wealthy— clean man." Lonnie looked past her, a smile stretching across his cheerful face. "Prepare to wade in grease, Stacy, here comes the next inter- ested man."

What Lonnie didn't say was that the interested man had called earlier. He was interested all right, but in buying the garage, not in its owner. And he was eligible. Lonnie had determined that from their conversation.

Stacy turned around. Her eyes fell on the man entering the shop. He was a meet-me-after-dark, lean, mean, good-looking stranger. There was only one problem. It wasn't dark, and she didn't think that he'd be open to a little flimflam. He was definitely a long shot.

Stacy sighed. She'd really gone out on a limb. But she wasn't the daughter of Lucky Lanham for nothing. He'd never been a welsher and neither was she. A bet is a bet, she told herself confidently as she caught sight of Lonnie's pleased expression and searched wildly for a way out.

There was none. Lonnie had obviously set this

up. She'd been outfoxed. She had to vamp this man—or make Lonnie think she had.

She'd maneuvered herself into a corner. Perversely she considered her options. She read the tabloids, about the escapades of women like Madonna and Cher. Vamping a man ought not to be too difficult. But after Lonnie's crack about the way she looked, she had to find a surefire way to get the man's immediate attention.

Just as the stranger reached the rack, Stacy stepped forward, closed her eyes, and gave a tug to the zipper of her coveralls, announcing with firm resolve, "I'm twenty-six years old. I'm not a virgin, but I'm available. If you're interested, state your terms, stranger."

The man stopped short and took in the woman who was turning from a caterpillar into a butterfly before his eyes. Beneath the gray coveralls she was wearing a soft, peach-color man's style old-fashioned ribbed undershirt and a matching pair of boxer shorts. Her soft brown hair, pulled up in a saucy ponytail only moments before, was unleashed and caught the late-afternoon sunlight, turning the color of fine brandy as it fell across her shoulders.

Peaches and cream, he thought crazily, feeling his lips relax and his tension release. Warm, spiced, cinnamony peaches and cream. She was like a pleasant balm that soaked up his tension. It took real effort not to curl his lips into a smile, and say, "Yum."

"I'm looking for Stacy Lanham." Gavin felt his pulse tap-dancing like raindrops on a tin roof.

"You're looking at her," Lonnie commented dryly, "at least a good part of her."

Stacy tried not to hear the amusement in Lonnie's voice. She only heard the pounding of her heart. The stranger was eyeing her quizzically. Had he said something? Was she expected to say something in return?

The stranger took a step closer.

She finally took a deep breath and blurted out, "So you want to deal?"

"Definitely. The name's Magadan, and my terms are either an outright sale or a merger." His mouth was spouting business phrases, but his eyes were sending messages that didn't bear translation into words.

"The name's Lanham. Let's get serious."

"Let's. I think I'm going to like the way you negotiate. Beats the hell out of either a chew of tobacco or lawyers and a conference room any day of the week."

On closer examination Stacy decided that she'd made a grave error. Clint Eastwood, move over. This was no ordinary man, no truck driver with a problem. Lonnie had really stacked the deck. The man was staring at her as if he were a bank robber and she were a role of greenbacks.

Beneath incredibly long brown lashes were the most intriguing pair of green eyes she'd ever seen. His dark hair was too long and too unruly to have been styled by a barber. With a speculative gleam he stared at her, appraising her leisurely. But it wasn't just the way he looked at her that stunned her, it was the way he dressed. Not many men came into the garage sporting a George Hamilton tan and a white polo shirt and white cotton pants. Not in Hiram, Georgia, in mid-July.

She knew that if she looked outside, she'd see a sports car—a long, sleek, white sports car—with a tennis racket tossed into the back and a workout bag on the seat.

He might belong on Rodeo Drive, maybe. Or in Hyannis Port, or at the Cherokee Country Club in nearby Atlanta. But not two blocks from the city dumpster, next door to Cecil's Farm Supply store, in the section just outside of Atlanta labeled redneck by one of the leading national magazines.

Gavin Magadan felt a rising admiration for the woman who wasn't a virgin but was available for a price. It was not quite the reception he'd anticipated when he'd come to buy her business. But Lonnie, the man he'd talked to on the phone earlier, had warned him that Stacy had a mind of her own and wasn't likely to give him the time of day. Gavin had had stranger offers and made deals that often contained peculiar conditions. This one, however, would be a first.

"Eh . . . eh, howdy," the bald-headed mechanic standing beside the girl interrupted belatedly. "I should have known better than to challenge Stacy. She's just like her daddy, he'd do anything to win a bet. Lonnie Short, here. Mr. Magadan, was it?"

"Gavin Magadan." Gavin shook the mechanic's hand, his gaze continuing to drift over the girl who brought the picture of peaches and cream to mind.

"Well, what about it, are you interested?" Stacy asked, waiting for Lonnie to admit his guilt and stop the bet.

"Absolutely," the stranger answered, and moved a step closer.

"Would you say that I'm vamping you?"

"I'd say you're making an attempt."

"What will it take to make it an all-out, state-of-the-art accomplished done deed?"

"Vamping me?"

"Vamping you. Lonnie bet me that I couldn't. I'm supposed to prove that he's wrong, Gatsby."

Gatsby? Not only was she nothing like what he'd expected, she had a sense of humor. This was becoming more and more intriguing. "More than you can accomplish in a garage with an audience," he answered, willing to go along with whatever fantasy the woman was creating.

"Will you sign a statement to the effect that I've succeeded?"

"If you'll consider what I'm offering in return."

"Done. Good night, Lonnie."

"But, Stacy," the old man argued, "I was only teasing. I don't know if he's really eligible. I really don't know him. He only came to talk about—"

"I'm eligible," Gavin said, silencing Lonnie effectively.

"You don't have to go through with it," Lonnie continued to argue. "We'll forget the bet. Forget about my week's pay."

"No way, Lonnie Short. Prepare to wade in grease. A Lanham never welshes on a bet. Besides, there isn't enough money in the checking account to pay you. This will make us even."

"But—but—" Lonnie protested in vain.

"Good night, Lonnie," Stacy said, stepping out of her coveralls and offering her hand to the stranger. "Let's go, Gatsby, if we still have a deal."

"We definitely have a deal. Where to?"

She opened the door to the battered wrecker and held it, wondering if he dared to plant those white pants on the smudged red vinyl seat inside.

"To a baseball game. Get in, Gatsby, I don't want to miss the end."

Gavin had been vamped in a lot of places, but a ballpark wasn't one of them. But then nothing about this deal was following the usual pattern. He'd expected to sit around awhile, chew the fat so to speak. Then he'd be asked to identify himself, where he was from, what his daddy did, and what kind of hunting dogs he had. Then, sooner or later, the dealing would commence. Buying this piece of property was going to be a different ball of wax.

Gavin looked at her confident smile and grinned in return, crawling inside the cab of the truck and pulling the door closed with a slam. "I'm all yours, darling."

Stacy moved around to the other side, climbed inside. "Lock up, Lonnie. See you tomorrow."

"Don't you want to know why I came?" her passenger asked curiously.

"Not really. If Lonnie had anything to do with it, I already know. Besides, everybody in Hiram saw you drive up. Your car will be locked up in my lot, and every move we make will be watched. Try anything, and the townspeople would have you strung up to the nearest tree before you could get past the county line."

Gavin gulped. He didn't doubt her words for a moment. "So, what do you have in mind?"

She started the engine. "All I want is your signature."

"I'm afraid that it comes with a price."

"Are you expensive?"

"Very."

"I never doubted it for a moment."

Stacy backed the wrecker out of the garage,

taking in the car parked outside. She'd been wrong. It wasn't white, it was red, bright red, and it wasn't a sports car, it was a classic 1952 Cadillac convertible. Ah, well, Gatsby in the nineties, she decided, and looked at her passenger.

He already sported a streak of grease on the knee of his white pants, and he'd planted his arm squarely on the window where Lonnie usually draped his sweat-wiping rags. She was beginning to feel a little sorry for Gavin Magadan. He'd been a good sport about playing along with the joke.

Her reason for driving off with him was a bit harder to justify. She and Lonnie were always playing jokes on each other, making outlandish bets which they went to great lengths to win, but this was the first time either of them had taken one to the extreme. She stole a glance at her victim and drew in a short grasp. He was staring at her. Against her will her gaze focused on his determined chin and strong mouth. There was something reckless about him. She'd known that the minute he'd allowed his devil-may-care answers to get him involved in Lonnie's bet.

Stacy had never seen a man more handsome, more out of place. Still, there was something about him that she understood, a carefree quality that she could identify with. He could give as good as he got. Bold, that was the explanation, she decided, that's what was making her pulse race and her skin feel as if she'd jumped into a vat of battery acid.

"Why?" she asked, fighting off the burning sensation centered about where the tab of her coverall zipper would have been if she hadn't stripped.

"Why, what?"

"Why'd you go along with Lonnie's gag?"

Because you make me feel good, wouldn't have made any sense, Gavin thought, even if he'd been honest enough to say it. But it was the truth. Her spontaneous smart talk had come so naturally that he'd found himself responding without hesitation. And before he'd realized what was happening he was returning quips of his own. She was fun, he decided, and fun was something he hadn't had much of, certainly not with a girl who ran a garage for eighteen wheelers and offered herself to a stranger on a bet.

Stacy Lanham was not only intriguing, she was falling right into his hands without his having to use subterfuge. He pushed aside the thought that he was taking unfair advantage of her and slid a pair of opaque sunglasses over his eyes. He leaned back with a satisfied grin and lazily stretched out his feet.

"Look out!"

But her warning came too late. His foot plunged through the floor of the cab into space, warm, windblown space that threw him forward into the windshield and forever destroyed his Hyannis Port whites.

Gavin brought his foot back to the solid section of flooring and looked ruefully at the jagged scratches on the side of his new Loafers. *So much for patting oneself on the back.*

"Sorry, I should have warned you about that hole. Guess the shoes were new, huh?"

"The shoes were new."

"Don't worry, I'll replace them."

"With Lonnie's paycheck money, the money that isn't in the bank account anyway?"

"Don't worry. I'm good for it."

"I'm counting on that. I wouldn't want to be

vamped by an amateur, and lose a good pair of shoes too."

"Uh-oh. Did I say I was an expert?" By this time Stacy was beginning to think she ought to explain it was all a joke. She should have established exactly what she'd meant by a vamping. The man who'd turned from the godfather into a character straight out of the Roaring Twenties seemed entirely too pleased with what was happening.

He was running his fingers through his carefully styled hair, and grinning. "The expertise of the vamping wasn't a condition of the bet, just the end result. What about a little side wager, to cover the price of the shoes? Double or nothing."

Stacy took a quick breath. If there was no money to pay Lonnie, there was certainly not enough to pay for a new pair of shoes. She had to think fast. "I never bet for more than ten bucks. What'd you have in mind?"

Gavin noticed the little twinge of worry that seemed to nag at the corner of her mouth. He wanted the advantage, but he didn't feel good about embarrassing her. From what he'd been able to find out in his background check on her, she was just what she appeared to be—open and honest, nothing like her father.

Gambling was something Gavin did every day of his life, in dealing with people, in making business deals that could earn or lose millions. But in this rattletrap of a wrecker, he was experiencing the pure pleasure of being with a woman who had the courage to be herself. And this time, he was gambling for himself, not some corporation that could afford to lose millions if the deal fell through. Gavin laughed, tightly at first, then more deeply.

"Hell, I don't know, we'll settle on something. Take me to your vamping place, if you're sure this vehicle will get us there."

"It'll get us there, Gatsby."

"Call me Gavin. I don't think I like the idea of playing Scott and Zelda. Theirs was a rather fatal attraction, don't you think?"

"Maybe, but they really lived their lives to the hilt. Don't you believe in taking a chance?"

Stacy didn't know why she was talking about taking chances. She sounded like her father, trying to justify some wild scheme with impossible odds. Certainly she never took real chances, at least she hadn't until now. She ought to turn around and drive back to the garage. But Lonnie might not have left yet, and she had no intention of letting him off the hook. For the last year he'd tried to match her up with every man from Atlanta to Hiram. Winning this bet, or making him think she'd won, ought to bring all his matchmaking to an end.

She allowed herself a big grin. Gatsby looked harmless, and she hadn't been far wrong with her warning about his being strung up. People looked after her, sometimes too well. And with Frankenstein and Dracula at home, Gavin Magadan, whoever he was, wouldn't be any danger to her. Besides, she had a ballgame to get to, and the only other place she could have taken him—Gene's Diner, in the middle of Hiram, Georgia—closed at two o'clock. She drove the one block that made up the long ago abandoned downtown of Hiram and took Sudie Road.

The best thing about her father's downturn in fortune was his moving away from the city into the little log house he'd built as a weekend getaway by the lake in the woods. At least the property was paid for. He'd called his retreat Last Chance and had erected a log portal announcing its name at the entrance.

"Last Chance?" Gavin said as they bumped down the gravel road. "Sounds ominous. Are you sure I'm going to be safe?"

"Absolutely. I never do away with the men I plan to vamp, at least not until afterward."

"That's good. I'd think a woman who wears men's boxer shorts and undershirts might be taking a chance. Say, you aren't into kinky games, are you?"

"Definitely, Gatsby. I wear boxer shorts because they're comfortable, and I like games." Stacy turned up a rutted drive to a log house and pulled into its carport. "This is it—Vamp Central."

Gavin started to crawl out of the truck, heard menacing growls of warning, and caught sight of two dogs from hell standing guard about two feet away. "Whoa!"

"Gatsby, I'd like you to meet my roommates. Stay, Frankenstein! Stay, Dracula! Now, you can get out."

"Are you sure? I don't mind losing the shoes, but the feet go so nicely with the rest of my body."

"They won't move unless I give the command."

"And what's the command? Just so I don't inadvertently set off a red alert."

"I think I'll keep that little bit of information to myself." She waited beside her sentries as he exited the truck, then turned into the breezeway that led from the carport to the house."

"What kind of dogs are they?" he asked, keeping as close as he could to her.

"Rottweilers. They belonged to my father. They're my protection."

"I don't guess you get many visitors."

"No, I don't." She could have said that he was the first man she'd ever brought to her hideaway. But that would have called for explanations, and she simply didn't have any, not for Gavin, or for herself.

Through the trees Gavin could see the diamond-studded water of a lake in the late-afternoon sunlight. Quiet, he thought, and safe. There were no street sounds, no people, no noise. She unlocked the back door and stepped inside, assuming that he would follow. He did.

So did Frankenstein and Dracula, carefully, menacingly, on silent feet.

She led him through a corridor into the combination kitchen and great room, then into a small room beyond which was obviously some kind of office or, on second look, a studio. From the bookshelf behind a desk she took a dictionary and opened it, running one finger down the listings.

"Here it is, *vamp—a noun, short for vampire: a woman who uses her charm or wiles to seduce and exploit men. Vamp, verb: to practice seductive wiles.* Well, I guess that's pretty clear."

"What, that you're going to seduce me, or drink my blood?"

"That depends on your conditions for the wager. Sit, Gatsby. Let's negotiate."

She walked back into the main room, pulled a maple captain's chair out from behind a round table stacked with paperback books. "Sit."

He complied. "Do I need a stenographer to take down the terms?"

"No, but a polygraph operator to test your honesty might be in order."

"Now, do I look like a crook?"

"No. Yes. Maybe. What does a crook look like, Gatsby?"

"The ones I deal with wear double-breasted suits and Italian shoes."

"The crooks in my horror novels have swarthy skin, big noses and carry semi-automatic weapons. And they belong to *the Family*. Like the Godfather."

"Then I'm safe. My only family is my mother and my aunt. My mother has silver hair and wears pearls, and my aunt . . . my aunt is a little harder to describe. Let's just say she is sixty-six and dresses like she's eighteen. Aunt Jane considers herself my mother's caretaker."

"Oh no, Jane? Baby Jane?"

He looked at the woman sitting across from him with a horrified expression on her face. "Baby?" He caught sight of the stack of Stephen King and Dean Koontz novels on the table. "*Jane?* Oh, as in *Whatever Happened to Baby Jane?* Are you a horror movie fan?"

"Sure. Next best thing to baseball. Where do you think I learned my vamping techniques?" Slowly and deliberately, Stacy moistened her lips with her tongue.

Then it hit him. *Short for vampire. Frankenstein and Dracula.* The woman hadn't been kidding. For just a moment he reacted to the crazy, illogical idea that she thought she was a vampire. He stood up, pushing his chair away from the table.

"Hell!"

Stacy groaned and sprang to her feet. "No, don't say that!"

From the hall came the ferocious growls of her protectors. He looked up as the first dog bared its teeth and lunged.

The dog's feet hit his chest. Gavin felt a hot tongue on his face just as his head hit the floor and the lights went out. He was dead. He'd been killed by two shades from hell. And all he'd wanted to do was buy Stacy Lanham's garage.

Two

Her handsome stranger was going to be licked to death before her eyes—either that or she'd be sued for harassment, lose the garage, and be forced to take up vamping full-time.

With a rottweiler planted on either side of his chest, slurping merrily, Gavin Magadan wasn't going anywhere, and Stacy felt safe in leaving her captive long enough to get an ampule of ammonia from the wrecker's first-aid kit.

She should have stopped the gag back at the garage. She'd gone along with the bet, intent on forcing Lonnie to confess on the spot. He hadn't. Then she'd expected the man in the white pants to explain himself. But he hadn't. Then she'd decided that Lonnie was probably trailing along behind them, ready to collect the minute that Gatsby signaled her failure.

Instead, Gavin Magadan had inadvertently given a signal to her dogs, the one signal the dogs would automatically obey, no matter who gave the command. And he'd been the victim of their response.

The sequence of events should have been funny. It wasn't. He'd hit his head and passed out. His clothes could be replaced, but a busted skull might not be so easily fixed.

Breaking the ammonia ampule beneath his nose, Stacy was rewarded with a groan and the startled look of green eyes that, when opened, probed like those of a Starship Android.

"What?" He pushed himself to his elbows, grabbing the back of his head as an obvious rack of pain brought a frown to his face. "Get those creatures away from me."

"Frankenstein! Dracula! Sit!"

Both dogs promptly obeyed, their bodies trembling in barely contained restraint, as if they knew very well that they'd performed their assigned duties satisfactorily and were waiting for their reward.

"Good boys! Are you hurt, Mr. Magadan?"

"I don't think so, but if this is a sample of your vamping technique, I don't think I can sign your certification of completion." He felt his neck with his fingertips, then blanched sheepishly as he realized what he was doing.

"Hey, I'm sorry about all this. I didn't mean for you to get hurt. I just wanted to scare Lonnie, once and for all. Where is he?"

Gavin let out half a breath, then held the rest as he took a good look at the woman hovering over him. All kidding aside, those same brandy-color eyes were stormy with real concern. A silver coin on a chain nestled in the crease between her breasts drew his eyes to the soft curves of her body. Her skin had the warm, blush color of one who spent a lot of time outdoors. And the woman actually had muscles, nice, curvy muscles that seemed perfect in her curvy body. Whatever she ate, she didn't skimp on meals. He decided that he'd never properly appreciated sleeveless ribbed undershirts. He'd never even worn undershirts, though he might have to change his mind.

"I don't know anything about Lonnie coming here."

"Don't kid me, Magadan. If it wasn't Lonnie, then who did put you up to this?"

Stacy was beginning to have doubts about the man she'd started off calling Gatsby. He really didn't look like one of the jaded rich that the nickname implied. He looked alive and intense, ready to take on the world, or, perhaps her, after what her dogs had done to him. In short, he looked bad.

Maybe the lick on his head had addled him. Maybe he really didn't know Lonnie. Maybe she'd truly opened herself up to a lawsuit. And she'd worried about something simple like replacing a pair of ruined white leather Loafers.

"If I had to put the blame for this on anybody," he finally said, "it would be my aunt, who is certainly going to be held accountable for the headache I have, not to mention possible broken ribs and whatever other injuries this 'lick' attack may have caused."

His aunt? Baby Jane? The man was definitely spacey. "Do you think you can get up?"

"Will the hounds from"—Gavin caught himself, remembering the last time he'd used that word—"*Hades* allow it?"

"They won't move until I give the proper command. Are you certain you're all right? You look a little pale, and I'm not sure you're thinking right. Maybe I ought to call a doctor."

Gavin decided that she might be right. It was the lick on his head that was making him have irrational thoughts about vampires and sunshine, instead of getting on with the task at hand— buying a seedy, run-down, small-town garage.

Stacy Lanham stood and held out her hand. From his position on the floor, the view of her legs was even more arresting than the close-up of the silver coin. His gaze started at her scruffy running shoes and swept upward, ending once more at the portion of her undershirt under which the coin had disappeared.

Gavin quickly took his captor's hand and came to his feet, viewing with dismay the multiple sets of black paw prints across his shirt.

Stacy let out a deep sigh. "Oh, dear. I'm afraid that I'm going to have to replace everything you're wearing."

"Is that standard vamping procedure?"

"Vamping? I'm very sorry. Vamping you was just a joke. I really don't know anything about vamping. I was just trying to teach Lonnie a lesson."

"By knocking me out and destroying my clothes?"

"No, by making Lonnie back off about my working in the garage. If you really don't know Lonnie, Mr. Magadan, I've made an awful mistake. If you'll go upstairs and take off your clothes, I'll throw them in the washer and clean them for you. It's the least I can do."

Gavin considered the offer, not in the light of clean clothes, but because he had never had such an afternoon. He could see their meeting coming to an abrupt end if he couldn't find a reason to prolong his stay. Buying Lanham's Trucking

Company and Fleet Garage was taking a backseat to his interest in its owner.

"Fine," he agreed as he started up the stairs, trying to remember what *he* was wearing underneath.

"Just throw them over the banister," she called out. "While they're washing, I'll find us something to drink and turn on—"

"Wine and music? Better and better," Gavin said under his breath.

". . . the game. The Braves are only a game and a half out and they're playing the Dodgers. Who do you like?"

"You," he said, knowing she couldn't hear. "Your peach-shaped breasts, your long legs, and your shapely bottom—" He fantasized as he removed his trousers and shirt. He was thinking orgy, and she was talking baseball.

Downstairs, Stacy turned on the television and listened to Ernie Johnson, former member of the broadcasting team who, though retired, came back now and then to fill in. She plundered through the closet in the utility room, looking for her father's favorite black silk robe. Lucky had called it a dressing gown and had said it made him look sophisticated. It had. If companies had used athletes as models when Lucky Lanham had played ball in the early seventies, he'd have been in the underwear advertisements.

Smith, the left fielder, got on with a single, and Pendleton got a hit. Stacy stood listening for a moment, holding the robe against her, thinking of the times she'd watched her father move the runners with his long, smooth hitting motion. Gavin's clothes sailed down from the loft bedroom, bringing her out of her spell of remembering, just as David Justice flew out.

Stacy held up the robe and considered the man she was about to give it to. At six feet, Lucky Lanham had been a big man, but Gavin was at least four inches taller. The robe might be short, but he could manage until his clothes were dry. Hearing footsteps on the stairs, she whirled around, ready to quiet the dogs who were still sitting where she'd left them.

"I'm—*leaving this robe on the stairs,*" she started to say, and swallowed her words.

Stacy looked up. He was wearing nothing but his white shoes and underwear. But his weren't boxer shorts, and they weren't casual facsimiles either. Magadan's underwear was made for X-rated movies, and the body beneath was protesting its constriction with every move he made down the steps.

"White?" she said without realizing she'd spoken aloud.

"Sorry, if I'd known I'd be the object of a vamping, I'd have worn something more—seductive."

At that moment a roar of crowd noise spilled out from the television in the great room behind. Stacy groaned. "A man scored. We're only one down with two innings to go. The manager will probably bring in a closing pitcher to hold them," Stacy said as if she were giving a play-by-play, all the while forcing her attention away from Gavin's body.

She tossed Gavin the robe and turned back to the television. She'd lost track of the outs in the shock of seeing the man's half-nude body. If the Braves lost their concentration as badly as she had, Lonnie was going to win both bets. Her vamping was no more effective than the Brave's starting pitcher's fast ball had been.

Gavin followed her, came even with the four-footed monsters, and cut his pace, expecting the black sentries to bar his path at any moment. They didn't. Only their tongues moved simultaneously as he threaded his way between them.

Stacy started up the washing machine, and the sound rumbled out from a room just beyond the kitchen. She took two cans of soft drinks from the refrigerator and motioned for Gavin to follow as she settled on the floor in front of the television and leaned back against the couch.

"About my coming to the garage," Gavin began.

"Shush!"

Gavin felt like a fool. He was standing in the woman's den, wearing nothing but his underwear, and she was actually watching a baseball game with the intensity of a ten-year-old playing an electronic video game. Disgruntled, he slid his arms into the black silk robe and looped the ties at the waist. Not only was he taller, but he was leaner than the man who originally wore this robe.

"What do you think, Magadan? Will they pitch to Olsen or walk him?"

"You're really serious about watching this game." Gavin walked around the couch and sat down on the floor beside her.

"Sure, I've got two dollars bet on it."

"Only two bucks? Doesn't seem worth the worry."

"That's why I'll win. I never lose."

"Really?"

"Really!"

"Then you're wasting your time on penny-ante stuff. Let's buy some lottery tickets, go to the dog track. Or, I know, Atlantic City. We'll give Donald Trump some real losses."

Gavin had only been kidding, until he saw the stricken look on her face.

"No. I never bet more than ten dollars," she said slowly. "Only for fun. Only with the guys. Only here, on little things that don't matter. I'm not a gambler, not really."

"But, Stacy, everybody's a gambler. Even life's a gamble. Nothing ventured, nothing gained." Then he thought of her garage and added, "If you intend to succeed."

"Depends on your definition of success, I guess. I believe that if a person finds his niche in life and doesn't try to be greedy, he'll survive."

"In other words, if you don't risk anything, you're safe."

"Something like that. You find your own fish pond and stay in it. Then you're okay. Nobody can hurt you if you don't let them."

The Dodgers starting pitcher didn't play it safe. He threw three straight strikes, hard and fast, right across the plate, and retired the side. Stacy let out a sigh of dismay and handed Gavin his soft drink. She gave a clucking sound, and the two dogs bounded into the room and collapsed on the floor beside her, laying their heads on their paws as if they were watching Gavin instead of the ball game.

"Do you like baseball, Magadan?"

"I'm afraid I'm not much of a fan."

"Somehow I could tell that. Tennis rackets, Cadillac convertibles, and white shoes don't go to the ball game. They go to the country club and to lawn parties, don't they? Where do you live?"

"I live with my mother and my aunt in an old section of Atlanta."

"With your mother? Now that's a kick in the pants. Sorry, bad pun, considering you aren't wearing any."

"I was beginning to think you hadn't noticed."

"Oh, I noticed all right. Now I understand why it's white—your underwear, I mean. I'll bet your mother bought it."

Gavin blanched. His mother had bought it. Not because he was some kind of mama's boy, as the smart-mouthed pixie watching the ball game implied, but because it gave her something to do with her time other than get involved in Aunt Jane's wild escapades. Though he didn't have enough clothes or money to totally prevent that.

"She did," he admitted with a grin. "Serviceable, white. I keep the black ones hidden under my mattress, with my *Playboy* magazines. What do you think?"

I think that I might be in big trouble. She'd tried to focus her attention on the game, but the thrumming of blood coursing through her veins had warmed her body to a heated pitch. She was beginning to have a fuzzy sensation, and she hadn't been hit on the head.

"I think, Magadan, that I'd better check on your clothes." She got to her feet. What she meant was that she'd better put some distance between herself and the man who looked better in Lucky's robe than Lucky ever had. But she stood rooted to the floor, her eyes glued to his casual stance.

The robe hit him about mid-thigh. His legs, crossed carelessly at the ankles, were as tan as his face. He might not run the bases, but he worked out, boy did he work out. She could see the muscles in his upper thigh pulsating as if they were answering her pulse rate with an SOS of their own.

"Unless you have the fastest washing machine on record, I don't think it's finished."

"Oh, I do. I mean, I put it on short cycle." Embarrassed at being mesmerized by his legs, she lifted her gaze to his face, taking in his amused smile.

"I like your legs, too, Anastasia Lanham. I like them very much. Don't worry. I would never want to be responsible for your losing a bet."

"What do you mean?"

"I mean, whenever you're ready, I say, let the vamping begin." He gave her a solemn wink and patted the floor beside him.

Her eyes flashed. The crowd noise on the television blared forth, and Gavin thought he'd been caught in a short circuit. Even he was amazed by the currents set off when their eyes met and stayed focused on each other. His head didn't pound, that was the wrong description of what was happening. He felt as if it were being invaded.

He watched Stacy's mouth fly open as she took in a deep breath of air, then let it out and gasp again. Her eyes were the color of hot brandy, and her face seemed to blush hotter, like a ripening peach in the summer heat. Then her eyes closed for a moment. When she opened them, they seemed to be begging him to stop, to release her from his hold. He blinked.

"Don't do that again," she whispered.

"What?"

"Whatever it is you're doing to make me feel so strange."

"I don't quite know how to say this, Stacy, but

whatever you're feeling, I'm feeling it too. Maybe you're doing a better job at vamping than either of us expected. Maybe I don't know how to turn it off."

The washing machine let out a beep and went silent.

The announcer on the commercial proclaimed that all a man had to do was use a certain deodorant, and women would swoon.

The dogs whined.

Stacy's eyes revealed her panic. Her mouth curved into a soft pleading shape, and she shook her head. "No."

The doorbell rang.

"Yes, Stacy."

The doorbell rang again, more urgently.

"Shall I answer the door?"

"No." She glanced from Gavin to the door and back again. "I mean, yes. I'll see about the clothes." She whirled around and disappeared before Gavin could come to his feet.

Gavin tightened the sash of the robe and went to the door.

Stacy pulled Gavin's shirt and trousers from the machine and groaned. She'd added bleach in a vain attempt to remove the grease. It had worked well, too well. The trousers hung in shreds. The bleach had removed the grease, and the battery acid had removed the fabric around the grease. The shirt was in slightly better shape. Now there was no question that she was in deep trouble. Tossing the tattered garments into the dryer, she forced herself to go back and confront the man who held her bank account, and therefore her future, in his hands.

She was wrong. It wasn't her future he was

holding, it was Lonnie's. And he was whaling away at Gavin like a hummingbird attacking a chicken hawk.

"You sorry, no-good, womanizing—" Lonnie, being held just out of reach, wasn't making contact with Gavin's bare chest. But that didn't stop him from trying.

"Lonnie! Stop! What are you doing?"

"I'm going to tar and feather him. Then I'm going to take him down to see Dr. Wingate, and we're going to alter his future life-style, without anesthesia."

"Mr. Short, if you'll stop, I'll try to explain."

"I'll bet you will, you lying son of a—you didn't come to buy Stacy's garage. You came to seduce Stacy. I'll see you in *hell*—"

"No!" Gavin shouted.

"No!" Stacy cried out at the same time.

Too late.

Frankenstein and Dracula caught Lonnie from the side, shoving him back out the door. They slurped him off the porch and into the yard.

"Stop it, you heathens!" Lonnie snapped. "Sit! I said, sit, or you'll be taking that trip to Dr. Wingate's along with us. He already said the next time you came for a bath that he's going to dip you in gasoline and strike a match."

The dogs sat. Apparently they were as accepting as their mistress, Gavin observed. They obeyed anybody who gave them a command. Some protection they would be if Stacy ever needed it. Lonnie came to his feet, his expression still murderous, his hands made into fists, and his arms extended in a challenge.

Gavin couldn't help it. He burst out laughing. "I take it Dr. Wingate is the local veterinarian?"

"Yes, and he raises and trains rottweilers." Stacy was having a hard time keeping her own lips from curling into a smile.

"If he trained these two specimens, I don't want him within ten feet of me. I trust his sense of humor even less than I trust his scalpel."

"Lonnie, stop scowling, and put down your hands. Mr. Magadan hasn't touched me."

"He hasn't?" Lonnie studied Gavin, taking in the silk robe, his disbelief slow to recede.

"He hasn't. I'm simply washing his clothes to get the grease out."

This time Lonnie's chortle was not for the robe, but for Stacy. He lowered his arms and relaxed his fingers. "You're washing clothes? The last time you washed clothes everything in the house turned pink. We never did get the stain out."

"Well, I got the grease out, Lonnie. I really did."

"And?"

"Do we still have that department store charge card?"

"Nope. You made me cut it up and put it in the garbage. Why?"

Stacy turned and walked back to the laundry, followed by Lonnie and Gavin. She opened the dryer door and took the pants out, holding them up by the only section of the trousers still in one piece, the band.

In silence the two men stared at the shredded white fabric.

"Well, no problem," Gavin said finally, "you already said you'd replace them."

"And I will, but it will take me a few days."

"Or months," Lonnie added.

Gavin took the trousers and dropped them in

the wastebasket beside the door. "Not necessary, gambling lady. I have a solution."

Stacy lifted her gaze. In the background she heard that another Braves runner had scored in the bottom of the ninth. The Braves had won. Therefore she'd won her bet. She never lost. That confident in-control feeling she'd lost earlier came back for a moment, then disappeared again as her gaze met Gavin's.

They were standing in a vacuum. The air was being squeezed out of the room, and the temperature was rising. Her pulse accelerated, and little spots of bright color floated across her vision. He was doing it to her again.

"What's your solution, Gatsby?"

"Come home with me and meet my mother and Aunt Jane, and we'll talk about a solution."

"Stacy," Lonnie interrupted, "the bet is over. Forget the vamping."

"Does Aunt Jane do the cooking?"

"I'll never try to find you another man," Lonnie promised, knowing that neither of them was listening.

"I never know what Mother and Aunt Jane will do, but I think you'll be pleased."

"When?"

"Tonight."

"I'd better not. I don't trust you. You make me feel very uncertain, and I don't like not being in control. And it's all your fault. You've done something to me."

Gavin had taken a step closer. "I think you're right. And maybe we'd better find out what."

"Ah, Stacy," Lonnie said in a worried voice. "Think about this. What would Lucky say?"

A long, strained moment passed.

Then Stacy smiled. Not a smile of pleasure, but of resignation. All the times she'd argued with her father, she'd always known when she'd reached the point where she had to give in. Whatever was happening between her and the long, lean man before her had to be resolved.

"You know what Lucky would say. He'd say, 'Go for it, Stacy.'"

Three

"You actually intend to drive home practically naked?"

"I do. That's why you're with me, so that if I'm stopped by the police, you can explain."

"They'd never believe the explanation."

"You take care of the Hiram Police, and I'll handle the City of Atlanta. I figure you owe me, after what you did to my clothes."

Stacy knew there were at least two dozen reasons why she shouldn't be in the Cadillac convertible with Gavin Magadan. At the top of the list was that she seldom went out to dinner with a man.

Not a man she'd just met.

Not a man who'd charmed her into wearing a dress for one of the few times in recent years.

Not a man wearing nothing but bikini underwear and a black satin robe.

She still wasn't sure how it happened. But here she was, with her hair flying in the breeze, her eyes squinting in the sun, and her lips chanting half-forgotten Hail Marys as Gavin drove. She refused to look at him. Looking at him just sent her into aftershock and made her do unnatural things, like agreeing to accompany him to meet his mother and his aunt Jane.

Gavin drove the Caddy with a sure but gentle touch. He got into the outside lane on the freeway and stayed there, refusing to look in his rearview mirror unless he couldn't avoid it. Seeing the two rottweilers sitting in the backseat as if they were the passengers and he was the chauffeur was more than he could abide.

Claw marks on vintage leather seats.

Dog hair on reproduced silver-threaded floor carpet.

Gavin shuddered. She'd put a spell on him. Somewhere between the vamping bet and the Braves' win, he'd taken a turn into *The Twilight Zone.*

But he couldn't keep his vow to keep his head facing straight ahead and get his mind together. The pull was too strong. He gave in and turned toward the woman who was hugging the passenger door handle as if she were drowning and the handle were a life raft. He still wasn't sure how he'd gotten involved with her.

Gavin Magadan, ladies' man extraordinaire, business tycoon, and entrepreneur had just gone to the garage to take an option to buy the property. The site was perfect, close enough to Atlanta to be identified with the city and far enough away to make the land affordable. The Lanham garage was the last piece he needed to fill in the sixty-acre site for the Magadan Classic Automotive Restoration Center—Magadan Classics.

Space had been allotted to handle every portion of automotive restoration from stock and reproductive parts, through the rebuilding of the engines, upholstering, and final painting of classic cars and trucks. One small shop would even specialize in bicycles and another in wheeled toys and vehicles. Gavin was giving some thought to a buggy shop to work with antique hansom cabs and stagecoaches. If it was manufactured before the seventies and moved people or goods, the Magadan Center would restore it.

The old expression that the only difference between men and boys was the price of their toys was the basis on which Gavin would make his fortune. Magadan Center, the most complete antique car restoration facility in the country, would be his. His million-dollar project was almost complete.

The site of Lanham's Garage would be the entrance to the center. Dealing with farmers and small businessmen was a long, drawn-out process, and he'd been certain that somebody would have warned Stacy before he got to her. Nobody had. He hadn't really worried about convincing her to sell. Her business was practically nonexistent, and she wouldn't be able to afford to turn down his offer.

But he'd spent the afternoon with her, more or less, and he hadn't even made an offer. Not only that, but he'd gotten lessons in baseball and dog training and a tongue-lashing from a crusty old mechanic who was as much in awe of Ms. Anastasia Lanham as Gavin had become.

Now he was taking her home to meet his mother and his aunt Jane, and he wasn't quite sure how that happened.

"Gavin?"

Her voice barely carried above the street noises outside the open convertible.

He turned to face her, and in that one split second he stopped wondering about the why and how of the situation. She'd called him Gavin. Not Magadan. Not Gatsby. He smiled, caught her hand, and drew her across the seat beside him. "Yes?"

"Back there, you said . . ." But she totally lost the thread of her conversation as he pushed his sunglasses on top of his head and turned moss-green eyes on her. Such a green. Like jewels, the kind kings conquered countries to claim. The worried expression on her face vanished, melting like ice in the sunlight.

"You can't talk in a convertible when the top is down," he yelled, "unless you sit close."

And if I sit close, I can't talk at all. Stacy chewed on her fingernail, looked down at its ragged edge and the permanent grease stain beneath it, and swallowed hard. She was twenty-six years old and acting as if she were fourteen. Still, there was something incredibly happy about the open car, the wind caressing her face, the man sitting beside her. He made her forget bills and dwindling customers and a future that grew more uncertain daily. He seemed to have the world in his grasp and the confidence to claim it.

There was something reckless about him that reminded her of the way her father came up with some far-out scheme to recoup his gambling losses. And, as she'd done a hundred times before, she automatically responded to that confidence. But even caught up in the wonder of the moment, Stacy had the presence of mind to question whether or not she could handle so much stress again. She was on a merry-go-round, and she didn't seem to be able to get off.

Before she had time to think, they were pulling off the expressway and driving past the Governor's Mansion, then down Valley Road. Stacy's eyes widened. When Gavin said he lived with his mother in an old section of the city, Stacy never expected the wealthy northside, or a house which looked like a castle on the cover of a Gothic novel. When he pulled around to the back and parked the convertible inside a carriage house, she knew that she'd made a big mistake.

The blue linen shirtwaist dress and sandals she was wearing were pure Hiram, Georgia, and there she was mere blocks from the Governor's Mansion.

"Gavin, I don't think this is a good idea." From between her breasts, she fished her lucky coin, the silver dollar that Lucky had given her so she could always call him, and planted it outside her blouse like a shield.

"You're wrong. This is a very good idea. And in about two minutes you're going to understand just how good an idea it is."

Before she could argue, the back door burst open and a tall, red-haired woman wearing a pair of cutoff blue jeans and a baseball cap dashed across the yard. "Gavin! Gavin! Lordy, she's perfect. Where did you find her? What's her name. Oh, my Lord, look Alice. She's wearing a talisman."

"Aunt Jane," he said, when she came to a pause, "this is Anastasia Lanham. She's come to dinner."

"It certainly is," Jane said in an intense voice.

"And she's descended from royalty too," Alice Magadan added in an agreeing whisper.

By this time Aunt Jane had turned away from Stacy and was sitting between Frankenstein and Dracula, hugging them alternately. "How extraordinary, how absolutely extraordinary. Not only is she perfect, exactly as I pictured, but she has her own bodyguards."

Alice Magadan stood beaming, as she looked from Stacy to Gavin and back. "You were absolutely right, Jane, about Gavin buying the land in Hiram, and now here's Anastasia, my future daughter-in-law, just as you predicted."

"Mother, Stacy's come to dinner, not to get married," Gavin said with pleasant resignation and a forgiving smile. "Don't mind them, Stacy, I told you they were a couple of eccentrics."

"Nonsense, don't pay any attention to my son. He's a skeptic. Come along, Anastasia. I want to know all about you." Alice Magadan took Stacy's hand and started toward the house.

Aunt Jane, accompanied by Dracula and Frankenstein, started across the concourse like Cleopatra on her barge.

After a few steps she paused, and commented over her shoulder. "I'm not sure where you left your clothes, Gavin, but we expect you to conduct yourself as a gentleman. We wouldn't want Stacy to think we don't know our manners. Come, boys, onward!"

Stacy realized she hadn't needed to worry about her simple linen dress. Alice was wearing a faded print silk dress, long out of date, but still lovely. Jane had changed into a flowing muumuu that seemed to have a stormy pattern of rain and lightning painted on a hot pink ocean. And Gatsby, the jaded playboy, had left her with his mother while he went to dress. When he returned, he was wearing tan trousers and a cream-color sweater that made Stacy think of pralines and ice cream.

Dinner with the Magadans was a child's wildest fantasy. Stacy finally decided that the only thing the two lovable women hadn't prepared was mud pies, though one sauce looked suspiciously like gooey red clay.

There was spicy fish wrapped in grape leaves from Madagascar, rice and fruit dishes from Thailand, and beans and tomatoes with pungent seasoning that she couldn't identify from Brazil. They drank green tea and tropical punch while sitting on the floor at small tables, and listened to oriental music that sounded like chimes in the wind.

After sampling and declining one of the dishes being passed, Gavin lifted his eyebrows in resignation. "Mother, would it be too much to expect something like spaghetti or corned beef and cabbage, or even plain old pot roast?"

"Why on earth would you want that when you can sample the delights of the world?" Jane said, bringing in a covered pewter tray. She leaned over Stacy's shoulder and swept the top from the platter.

Visions of *Whatever Happened to Baby Jane?* washed over Stacy as she caught sight of the uncooked, white-skinned bird glaring up at her. She let out a half-aborted shriek.

"Hell-*o*" Gavin said, and came to his feet, realizing what he'd almost said in time to yell at the dogs rushing toward him. "Sit! Sit, you worthless creatures, or I'll let Aunt Jane barbecue you."

The dogs complied. Alice laughed and clapped her hands, while Jane glanced at the pheasant curiously. "Well, maybe it could use a little browning," she agreed, and headed toward the kitchen.

"I tried to tell her that olives and fish was quite enough for the main dish," Alice said, "but you know your aunt when she makes up her mind."

With that statement she dismissed Gavin and the dogs and turned back to Stacy. "Now, tell us about your garage, dear. When do you expect to close it down?"

Stacy felt as though she were having lunch with the Mad Hatter. She expected any minute to disappear through the rabbit hole and reappear in her little log house overlooking her quiet lake.

"Close the garage?"

In the mirror opposite the dining area Stacy caught sight of Gavin vigorously shaking his head.

"I don't understand." She turned to Gavin. "That's the second reference I've heard to the garage. Do you want to explain?"

"It's quite simple, I want to buy it."

"And my answer is equally simple: I don't want to sell."

"I know. I'm prepared to negotiate."

"Is that why you brought me here?"

"Certainly not. I don't even want to talk about your garage now, Stacy. Later, when I've had a chance to go over all the details, I'll tell you about my plans. For now, it will take all our wits to get through dinner. What is this green stuff, Mother?"

"Poke Soufflé. We decided that if a soufflé could be made from spinach, it could be made from pokeweed. Just think what a boon that would be to the homeless. All they'd have to do is go out and pull up some poke. It grows along every underpass and railroad track."

"Good idea, Mother. But where do you expect them to get the eggs?"

"Oh, dear. It's not such a good idea, I guess, unless they have chickens. I suppose chickens in downtown Atlanta would be against the law. Officials are so tacky about those things."

"We'll have to work on the recipe," Jane admitted, grimacing as she came out of the kitchen. "I think it needs a little something. I decided to save the pheasant for tomorrow. Pheasant under Pewter ought to be as good as Pheasant under Glass, provided I remember to turn the oven on."

After a surprisingly ordinary dessert of Key Lime pie, they adjourned to the study for coffee.

"Do you think you're going to like being a millionaire's wife?" Alice asked pleasantly.

"I'm quite sure I don't know, since I'm not getting married and I haven't met any millionaires."

"Oh, but Gavin is almost there, or at least he will be by his thirty-first birthday," Jane chimed in. "I know he's disappointed that it's happening a year late. But I say it's better late than never. Don't you?"

"What my mother is trying to say, Stacy, is that I always said that I'd be a millionaire by the time I was thirty. I was thirty last September."

Stacy looked around. Everything was happening so fast that she couldn't begin to absorb it all. Twelve hours earlier she'd been putting new plugs in Larry Greenway's gravel truck. Six hours earlier she'd made a bet on a Braves' baseball game.

Now there she was, in a house so fine, she was afraid to walk on the carpet, eating strange dishes as if she'd been doing it all her life, and obviously being brainwashed in some weird way that she couldn't understand.

"You may not be a millionaire," she sputtered, "but from the looks of this I'd say that you don't need to worry too much about how you're going to pay the light bill."

"Oh, we're not worried about the power bill this month," Jane reassured her. "The tarot cards said we'd see the light, so I paid the telephone bill instead. But don't try to use the hot water."

"I'm afraid to ask, Aunt Jane, but I guess I'd better know. Why can't we use the hot water?"

"Well, it's just that there wasn't enough money in the checking account to pay the power company, the gas company, and the telephone bill. So I decided that since we could always heat the water, I wouldn't worry about the gas bill. I paid the water bill instead."

Gavin walked back to his chair and sat. "Why isn't there enough money in the checking account, Aunt Jane? I just made a very large deposit. It was to last you until I get the loan approved for the center and get my option money back."

"I—we—we spent it."

"On what? Not more exotic animals?"

"Oh, no. We understand now about residential zoning laws. We gave the creatures to the zoo. But I did hate to give up the camel."

"Then what? Mother? What have you done with the money?"

"We've taken a lease on a building. The same as

you're doing. We decided to open our own center, a spiritual center."

Stacy heard Gavin groan. She was holding her lips pressed together with difficulty. Any minute she was afraid she'd break into laughter, and she didn't want the dear old ladies to think she was making fun of them.

"What kind of spiritual center, Mother?"

Alice beamed even more. "We're calling it the *Center for the Spiritual Odyssey of Man,* and women, too, of course. We don't intend to discriminate. We'll give readings, counsel the troubled, and serve tea and peanut butter. That's full of protein, you know."

"And best of all," Jane chimed in, "we'll be right where we can do the most good."

"I'm afraid to ask. Where?"

"Right in the middle of downtown Atlanta. That way we can reach out to the downtrodden and confused, those poor homeless people who need our help so desperately."

Stacy couldn't hold it in any longer. She laughed, covered her mouth, and asked, "Have you considered offering bingo on Friday nights? And you could offer fasting one day followed by free food the next."

Gavin studied Stacy with a half-veiled expression in his eyes that registered his surprise.

"What a very good idea," Alice said, nodding her head. "Jane, you were so right. She's perfect for us, and Gavin will come around as soon as he sees how well the three of us get on."

This time his mother and his aunt had gone too far. Gavin still wasn't convinced that Aunt Jane had any sort of psychic power or ability to foresee the future. But he had no other explanation for whatever had come over him with Stacy this afternoon. Aunt Jane had sent him to Stacy. Well, not Stacy specifically, but she'd made some vague reference to an old friend who'd once bought a garage in Hiram because the land was cheap. Then, Gavin had taken one look at Stacy and melted. The next thing he knew, he'd practically shanghaied her and brought her home to meet Jane and Alice.

Nothing made sense. From the moment his eyes had met Stacy's something had turned his mind into putty and painted his nerve endings with wild, uncontrollable urges. Even now his skin was tingling.

Past experience told Gavin that asking Jane for explanations only made things more confusing. He'd have to figure it out—and quick—or poor Stacy would be so confused that he'd lose the garage and her as well.

"Speaking of people getting along, Mother, it's time I took Stacy home, before she runs out of here screaming."

"She isn't going to do that, are you darling? You understood right away about our grand idea, didn't you?"

Stacy let out a long, deep breath and nodded as she allowed Gavin to take her hand and draw her toward the door. "Oh, yes. I understand. After all, I lived with plans just like these most of my life."

"Lucky you," Jane said softly.

"No, not me. Lucky was my father, and he was anything but."

"Lucky?" Alice looked up quizzically. "Jane, didn't you know someone called Lucky once? A big, tall man with grand ideas. He was an athlete of some kind, if I remember right. Terribly handsome man. Right after you invested in his ice-skating rink it burned down, and he just disappeared."

"He died," Stacy said. "Lucky Lanham was my father."

Now Stacy understood. All this was happening because of her father. She should have known, but it had been a long time since one of Lucky's failed schemes had come back to haunt her. The lovely Magadan women fit Lucky's pattern— wealthy, gullible, and charming. She'd been down this road before. But Gavin was an unknown factor.

"Lucky Lanham, imagine that, Jane. At least we know he didn't desert you. He died. No wonder he never made it back for the wedding."

"I knew, Alice. You always thought it was because he found out that I had no inheritance. But I always knew better. Poor Lucky. I scared him to death. He was a lover, but marriage wasn't in his plan. That was all right. It wasn't in mine either. But the cards did say he'd die with his boots on. Did he? Have his boots on?"

"Yes, he did," Stacy said, still in shock over learning that Aunt Jane had thought her father was going to marry her. After her mother died, Lucky became a confirmed bachelor. And if you could call having a heart attack while making love to a twenty-one-year-old jet-setter dying with your boots on, then Lucky had finally gotten lucky.

He'd always joked that he'd won Stacy in a poker game, from a woman who'd had six children and two pairs. Stacy knew better. Her mother had been hit by a drunk driver when Stacy was six. That was when Lonnie and his wife had come into Stacy's life as her caretakers. Lonnie had been there ever since. Lucky had been harder to keep up with, and finally she'd stopped trying.

Stacy always thought that if Lucky could have made a bet on his demise, he might have dreamed up just such a way to go—in bed, in action.

Later, in the convertible, she sat quietly, leaning against the seat, letting the frantic pace of the evening dissipate in the soft summer air.

"You know, Magadan, we're going to have to make some sense out of all this, sooner or later."

"I won't make any promises. I've been trying to do that for thirty years and haven't succeeded yet. Couldn't we just forget my family? Alice and Jane drive me crazy, and I've lived with them most of my life."

"I don't doubt that for a minute. But they're nice. I like them."

Gavin knew he ought to bring up buying the garage, but he didn't want to talk business. He didn't want to talk about his family. He wanted to be with Stacy. But Stacy seemed wary. Somehow she'd lost her confident air. Even the dogs whined nervously in the backseat.

"We still have to take steps to settle your bet," Gavin finally said.

"What steps?"

"The certificate of completion of the vamping. Tonight I'd just like to enjoy being with a beautiful woman. Couldn't we just be the vamp-*er* and vamp-*ee* for now?"

"Beautiful woman?"

Stacy's voice was incredulous. Gavin suspected that she'd been called many things in her life, but beautiful wasn't one of them. She gave a chortle as if she were waiting for the pitch that was sure to follow.

Overhead a sleek, silver-dollar moon followed along as they rode. It was a night for lovers, or, if he were a horror fan, he might say for creatures on the prowl. She hadn't responded to his quip about the vamping. Maybe he'd approach her from another direction. Gavin smiled and touched Stacy's shoulder.

"Do you feel it?"

"What?"

"The power of the night when the creatures of darkness come to life." He caught her attention, and he watched a kind of liveliness sweep over her as she turned to face him. That was all he wanted.

"Look, Stacy, look at the moon. I want you to know that I'm prepared to be vamped, or metamorphosed. It's your choice."

"I don't understand what you're talking about, Magadan. I'm not really into vamping. What do you expect me to do?"

"As I recall there were several vamping definitions in that dictionary. If you don't want to seduce me, well—how do you feel about coming over here and biting my neck?"

Four

"This isn't Translyvania, Magadan."

"I know. But according to your sign, it's my last chance, And I intend to do whatever it takes to live forever."

"Vampires went out with Bela Lugosi and George Hamilton. Freddie, Jason, even Edward Scissorhands are today's night creatures."

"Personally, I'm more into Bill Murray and *Ghostbusters*."

The dogs suddenly growled, their ears pricking in recognition as the convertible turned into the gravel road leading to Stacy's house.

"No offense, boys. I like monsters and vampires, too, when they're in their place—which isn't the back of my car." Gavin turned off the engine and sat in the darkness for a few minutes, wishing that he could sort out his conflicting emotions.

Stacy was the first woman who'd ever met his mother and his aunt without wondering if they were suffering from drug or alcohol abuse, or some kind of harmless age dementia. Normally he tried to keep the two apart when others were around. Separation seemed to subdue them. Together, they fed off each other, and he never knew what they'd do. But Stacy had fallen into their half-finished sentences and half-thought-out schemes as if she'd lived with them always. They'd claimed her, and he'd been the one left out.

Finally, in fear of losing her to them completely, he'd spirited Stacy away. He was still shaking his head over his mothers invitation to Stacy to stay the night, which had been issued after the conversation about Lucky. Sounding very worldly, Alice had explained that she understood about the changes in life-styles and implied that she would accept any relationship Gavin and Stacy cared to enjoy. In fact, Aunt Jane had taken him aside and cautioned him about being prepared. He wasn't certain that Stacy understood what was happening, and he wondered what she would have done if he'd gone along with his aunt.

"You're the first woman my mother has invited to spend the night."

"Your mother and your aunt are darlings, Gavin."

"I don't think you quite understand. I think what they were saying was that they approved of us sharing my bed."

Stacy jerked her head away from Gavin's shoulder where it had somehow ended up on the drive home, and sat up straight. "Sorry, I guess I missed that."

"I'm sorry I will, too," Gavin confessed, trying to push the thought of her sharing his bed from his mind.

Now that the evening was over, Stacy was beginning to have grave doubts about everything that had happened. She felt as if she'd been caught up in an emotional whirlwind that had suddenly stopped. She felt drained, and very weak. If she stood, she might not be able to walk. For almost eight hours she'd tried not to think about what was happening. She thought she just might *have* vamped a man. Though she wasn't exactly sure, and she knew she would rather die than ask. The only thing she was sure of was that she'd won her two-dollar bet.

Except winning had taken on a different meaning. There in the darkness it hit her—not the normal excitement of winning—but the knowledge that everything had changed. The change, and the man responsible for it, were things she didn't know how to deal with.

As if he understood her confusion, Gavin searched for a way to change the focus of the moment. "Don't you ever get lonely out here?"

"No, not so far. There are the dogs, and Lonnie, and—friends."

"Men friends?"

"Sometimes, yes. They watch the ball games and horror movies with me." She didn't know why she felt the need to explain, but she did.

Ah yes, he thought, those horror movies. He reached out in the darkness, touched her face, and felt her flinch. "Have I spooked you?"

He hadn't, until his fingertips rimmed her ear and brushed a strand of hair behind it, then slipped to the back of her neck and pulled her gently into the hollow of his arm.

"Don't. I don't want you to touch me, not anymore, not until I find out what you're really asking of me."

"I fear that what I'm asking now and what I started out asking are vastly different."

"Start with what you had in mind when you came to the garage—the truth."

He didn't want to talk about that, and yet it was too important to ignore. Still, he sensed that once she found out what he really had in mind, what they were feeling would be reduced to money, and money was no longer the most important thing in his world. "Will you let me come in?"

She pulled away from his touch and immediately regretted her action. Suddenly the night was cool and alien. She'd never missed a man's touch before. The heat, the sensation seemed to sizzle and die like a fire doused with water. She'd lost more than a bet. She'd lost her common sense too. And with it had gone her sense of security. She felt as if she were heading in a direction she wasn't sure she wanted to go in, but she was powerless to stop herself.

These things didn't happen in real life, only in Ingrid Bergman movies, where people met in some mysterious, foreign place and were instantly linked for all times. One kiss and they were connected. Except Gavin hadn't kissed her. Only their gazes had met and locked. Only his touch had made heated images on her skin.

"All right, Magadan," she said with a sigh, "but you can't stay."

He wasn't Gavin anymore. But he wasn't sure why the change bothered him. He wasn't good with long-term involvements. His relationships tended to be intense, heated, and short. But he didn't want to frighten Stacy. He reached down to find an approach he thought might make her feel more comfortable.

"We're both gamblers, Stacy. What do you say we make a little wager on that?"

She opened the door and slid out, pulling forward the seat so that the dogs could dash ahead. A warning bark from each of them, and they disappeared into the darkness.

"I've given up betting," she said softly as she reached above the door frame to locate the key.

He took it from her, his fingertips brushing hers, then opened the door and followed her inside. "So, we'll play a quick game of Scrabble. Winner makes the choice."

"I don't have a Scrabble game."

"And I don't really want to play." Gavin took his time. He didn't make any sudden moves. Stacy had turned on the kitchen light and was leaning against the counter, wide-eyed and wary, her arms crossed over her chest.

"First we talk business. Then I'm going to kiss you."

"You're what?"

"Then later, I'm going to buy your business, Stacy Lanham."

"Why?"

"Because I need it." *It, the business,* was what he implied. What he really meant was *the kiss and you.* Slowly he moved closer, taking her arms in his hands.

"Gavin, somebody gave you a bad tip if they told you the garage was worth anything. I wish it was. But it isn't."

"Not as it stands, but in a year your garage will be the entrance to the Magadan Classic Automotive Restoration Center—Magadan Classics, for short."

"No it won't. The garage is all I have left, and I have no interest in selling it."

"But I'm willing to give you a good price, more than it's worth."

"I don't doubt that for a minute. But, no."

"Why?"

"Because it's mine. And I don't have anything else. What would I do?"

"The answer to your question has to do with my second offer—this." The honorable part of him knew that he was taking advantage of her vulnerability. She'd never before been with anyone whose very touch melted her. But then, neither had he.

Gavin knew he ought to pull back, ought to state his case logically so that she'd understand. But his own need was greater than his control, and when he lowered his head, he could see that she wanted him to kiss her. Her lips parted, first in a gasp, then in soft compliance as they met his.

The air was charged. A low murmur slipped out of her, and he moved one hand from her arm to her cheek, gently steadying her as his tongue teased her mouth, opening it as if he were tasting her.

He watched her face change. The tension was replaced with a tentative smile, followed by an almost inaudible moan. Instinctively she cocked her head, and he felt a wave of pleasure ripple through her. She was a dream, his secret night dream, the woman who came to him in those moments of insecurity that he'd always managed to mask with brash abandon. As her arms slid around his waist and she moved shyly against him, he felt a great answering longing in himself.

In Gavin's arms Stacy could feel the beat of his

heart, the slow, steady building of desire that cushioned her fears and then erased them touch by touch. The kiss deepened, pushing them further from reality. It became filled not just with passion but, in some indefinable way, with a promise of tomorrow, and Stacy lost the last of her resolve.

For all her life she'd waited for this moment. If someone had told her, she would have denied it. But now she knew, and that knowledge spun outward in a web of heat that infused her body with desire and her heart with the sure knowledge that this moment was right.

A *fantasy*? Yes, Gavin acknowledged.

A *miracle*? Probably, but to Stacy it no longer mattered.

"Stay," she whispered. "Stay with me tonight." She couldn't look away from him. The connection was overpowering, intoxicating.

Gavin had one hand on her breast. The other was pressed against her back, holding her in a vice that might have frightened her if she hadn't been returning his kiss with abandon. Her lips were searching, responding so completely that he had great difficulty holding on to his last shred of reason. He wouldn't have stopped. He couldn't have stopped, if it weren't for a recurring sound in the silence.

The dogs. They first scratched on the door, then set up a whine that turned into a howl that wiped away the cushion of desire protecting them from the outside world.

"Your guardians are calling, darling."

"Tell them to sit," she whispered. "Stay. Go away."

"I don't think they hear you."

"Ignore them, Gavin."

But the howling continued until it couldn't be ignored by either Gavin or Stacy.

Finally Gavin pulled away and shook his head slowly. "I think I'd better go, Anastasia Lanham, before I do something that might spoil whatever we have going here."

"You know you don't have to."

"I know, and that's why I have to leave. I think I want to come back again."

"Why?"

"I want to go to a baseball game with you. I want to take you to a parade. I want—you, Stacy, and the only way I'll get you is to let you go for now."

He let her go. Stacy felt herself sway. Like a blade of grass in the wind again, she thought, and shuddered with longing. "Gavin?"

"Yes?" He took a deep breath. Her beautiful face was flushed. The front of her dress was open, and he could see the rise and fall of the dainty white lace covering her breasts as she breathed.

"I have a little bet with myself. Satisfy my curiosity."

The thought of satisfying her swept his breath away, and it took him a ragged moment to refocus on her words. "I think—I'd like very much to do that, Stacy. What can I tell you?"

"What color is it?"

"Color?" He tried to collect his thoughts, but the only picture in his mind was Stacy in his arms, in his bed.

"Your underwear? Is it still white, or were you prepared to be vamped?"

She broke the spell with her smile and her question. She was talking underwear, and he was talking climax. "Prepared? Oh, lady, I'm so prepared that unless I get out of here quick, your dogs may mistake my sweeping you up in my arms for an attack on your person. He turned way, forcing himself to walk to the door.

He could hear her following. He pushed open the screen door and let the monsters inside. They took their places on either side of Stacy and glared at Gavin as if to say they knew what was in his mind, and they intended to make certain that it didn't become a reality.

"You didn't answer me, Gavin."

"And I don't intend to, Stacy Lanham. That's a question for another night."

He walked across the porch and down the path to the car, feeling the torture of his arousal announcing itself with every step. There were some things a woman didn't need to know. There were some mistakes a man could make in the name of desire. Some mistakes a man only made once.

The truth was, if she'd done any investigating, she'd have known that he wasn't wearing any underwear at all.

Lonnie couldn't hold his questions any longer. "So, Anastasia, are you going to tell me what happened? Or are you just going to bounce off the ceiling all morning like some hot-air balloon.

Stacy wasn't exactly sure what she'd intended to do this morning. But the only thing she'd managed to do was flip through the bills. They hadn't seemed important somehow.

"Did you know that Lucky knew Gavin's aunt?"

"Lucky probably knew most of the women in the Southeast and a good portion in the rest of the country as well. What was her name?"

"Jane. You know, I never learned her last name. But she invested in an ice-skating rink that Lucky was backing."

"Oh, yes. I remember. It burned down. Jane, you say?"

"Yes. Red hair. What I guess you'd call a free spirit."

"Yep. I remember. She was the one. He got too close to the fire, and he ran away like a wounded dog. I always wondered if he burned down the rink himself, and if he did, whether it was to escape from his creditors or his feelings."

Stacy cut her eyes to her old friend. "What do you mean? How does somebody burn down an ice rink anyway?"

"I don't know. I wasn't there. I only know that for a week Lucky acted a lot like you are this morning. He seemed two miles high and with all his faults, Lucky didn't do drugs. The rink was new, and he stood to make a bundle. Next thing I knew the building was gone, and Lucky left the state. I always thought he got a little singed in the deal, but it was a long time before I figured out it was the woman with the money, not the fire, that got to him. He always intended to hit it big and pay her back, but he never did."

Through the years Stacy had been faced with settling many of Lucky's debts. But this one came as a disturbing surprise. Jane had invested in one of her father's schemes and lost. And she'd never pursued the return of her money. Ironic? Or was this some kind of delayed plan on her part to recoup her losses. Gavin had said that his coming to Hiram was Aunt Jane's fault.

Just as I knew she would be. That's what Aunt Jane had said when they'd met. The unshakable euphoria that had followed Stacy all morning suddenly vanished and she came crashing back to reality.

"That explains it, Lonnie. Lucky cheated Gavin's aunt out of her money, and somehow she found me. I'm part of a plan for revenge. What am I going to do?"

"What has Aunt Jane got to do with Magadan buying your garage. If they were out to get you, they'd take it. If what he told me is even half true, you're going to stand to make a pretty profit on this deal."

"I don't know, but I'm going to find out."

Stacy had started toward the office when her progress was halted by a crashing sound and a blow. The grinding didn't stop until the perpetrator slammed off the side of the building and into the garage.

"Oh, my goodness, Jane. I believe you hit something." Alice's voice didn't really seem disturbed as she added, "Gavin's going to be dreadfully angry. We should have waited until he got back with the Buick."

"Then he'd have known we came."

"I believe he's going to know anyhow."

Stacy knew that Gavin had been greatly disturbed last night about the dogs riding in his backseat. As she took in the damage to the front fender of his prize antique car, she decided that his earlier fears were futile. What his mother and his aunt had done to his car was indescribable.

Lonnie gulped and stepped forward. "Are you ladies all right?"

Alice opened the passenger door and got out. By the time she walked around to the front of the car,

Jane had joined her. They studied the damage, glanced at each other, and looked back at Stacy.

"Well, my dear," Alice explained. "We tried to figure out a good reason to come to call on you so soon, a reason that wouldn't anger my son—"

"Yes. You know he doesn't like us to muck about in his business," Jane interrupted.

"But I don't think this is exactly what we had in mind. Do you have someplace I could sit down?"

Stacy brushed off her shock and went forward. With her and Lonnie assisting Alice, they managed to get the woman inside the office.

"Can I get you a glass of water?" Lonnie asked, lifting a cone of paper cups from atop the file cabinet.

"Yes, that would be nice," Alice said faintly, reaching for her monogrammed linen handkerchief.

"Sure, and pour a shot of this in it." Jane uncapped a silver flask she carried in her tapestry purse and handed it to Lonnie. "In fact, pour us all a shot."

Lonnie filled the cups, added Jane's stimulant, and swallowed his in one gulp before he turned to Stacy. "I take it these are Gavin's ladies?"

"Yes, and I don't think he's going to be too pleased with what's happened. Aunt Jane, why did you come to see me? If it's about the money, I don't know what I can do right now. But I'll find some somewhere."

"Money?" Jane raised her eyebrows in question. "What money? I'm afraid I don't have any. But I'm certain that Gavin can help you. He's promised to be very generous in his offer for your garage."

"Then it's true?"

"Of course it's true. My nephew would never

cheat anybody. He'll pay you a fair price. You can just consider it your dowry and put it away. He'll support you properly, I promise."

"My dowry?"

"Jane, I think you ought to let Gavin and Stacy work out their own plans. What we came to tell her is that we approve, and that we're going to move into the loft of our new building so that they can have the house to themselves."

Lonnie emptied the flask into his paper cup and took a gulp as he collapsed on a stack of crates near the door. "I hope this makes some kind of sense to you, Stacy. I'll be doggoned if I understand a word they're saying."

"I've got the answer, Alice. Lordy, it's perfect. Stacy and—what is your name, sir?"

"Lonnie Short, ma'am."

"And Mr. Short will repair the car," Alice completed the sentence, adding, "That will work perfectly, Jane."

"Mrs. Magadan," Stacy said, "we can't repair this car."

"Why not? This is a garage, isn't it?"

"Yes, but we only work on trucks."

"But the only difference between a truck and a car is one's big and dirty, and the other isn't," Jane observed. "Besides, you don't look too busy at the moment. We'll just leave a deposit, and Mr. Short can drive us home." She took out a bill and handed it to Lonnie.

Lonnie looked at the money and shook his head. "Damn! This is a hundred-dollar bill."

"You're right. That isn't enough? Do you have any money, Alice?"

"Ladies, this is far too much. I have to tell you, the battery on the truck is down, and the only vehicle I have to drive you in is a wrecker. I don't think a wrecker belongs in your neighborhood."

"Nonsense," Alice corrected. "A wrecker will be great fun. Besides, Jane, didn't the cards say we were going to take a journey?"

"You're right. Shall we, Mr. Short—Lonnie?" Jane offered the bemused Lonnie her arm, and they walked out of the office toward the big red truck with Alice following behind. Alice was beaming again, as if everything had worked out just as she'd planned.

Stacy watched them get up into the cab. She watched Lonnie back out, pass the crumpled Cadillac, and drive away. She stood there wondering how she was going to get herself out of the explosion she was sure was about to happen.

Suddenly, as if on cue, the lights flickered and the crumpled fender creaked and sagged to the concrete garage floor. Then the world went silent in the too empty, lifeless garage.

Stacy decided that she'd been hexed. Some sorcerer or evil witch had put a spell on her and everything around her. She felt as if she were taking part in the Friday cliff-hanger of a soap opera. She was falling over the edge. The rope was breaking, and she was about to drop into the pit of boiling oil. Disaster was heading her way, and there was nothing she could do to avoid the eventual outcome.

Stacy caught her lucky coin and began to rub it between her fingers. "If you've ever been lucky for me," she pleaded, "be lucky now."

The answering screech of brakes in the yard beyond told her that whatever luck she'd had, had just run out.

Five

"Mother! Aunt Jane! Where are you?"

Gavin Magadan strode into the shop, caught sight of his convertible, and stopped dead. He felt like crying, but a man didn't cry.

"Oh, no!"

Stacy swallowed hard. She could see the disbelief on Gavin's face. She could see him make a valiant attempt to hide it as he scanned the garage in search of his mother. Instead, his gaze found her.

"Are they all right?"

"Yes," Stacy whispered, surprised by an unexpected need to put her arms around him, to comfort him, to tell him that she understood. Stacy knew that it was just a car, but to Gavin it was more. He'd taken something that had been broken, discarded, and had brought it back to life. "Lonnie took them home. How'd you know they were here?"

"Years of trying to stay ahead of them. I knew that they'd come. I just don't understand," Gavin confessed. "They've never taken my car before. In all their crazy schemes and ideas, they've understood about the car. In fact, the restoration center was Aunt Jane's idea. Why?"

"Why did they take your car? I don't know. But I think the brakes failed, and they clipped the building." Stacy edged closer. This time she did reach out and touch his face, to comfort and share. "It can be repaired, Gavin."

"Do you know how hard it is to find antique Cadillac car parts?"

"No, but I'm a pretty fair mechanic. I can handle the brakes, and Lonnie knows more about bodywork than anybody I know." She slid her hand down across his shoulder, down his arm and gripped his hand.

"I guess I don't have any choice, do I? I'll get on the phone with Jim, my parts man, and see if we have a fender. I have to get this car repaired."

But Stacy could tell that Gavin wasn't satisfied. No matter what nonsense his aunt and mother had spouted last night about paying bills, Gavin could obviously afford to buy a new car, if he needed one.

"Why is this car so important, Magadan?" she finally asked.

"Because I'd agreed to sell it to—it doesn't matter. I'll have to think of something else to satisfy them."

"You're going to sell your car? Why? You obviously care a great deal about it."

"I do. But I care about the center more. The man who loaned me the money for the options on the land wanted the car, and I had to agree, or he wouldn't have given me the loan."

"He doesn't sound like any banker I ever heard

of. I thought the land itself would be the collateral for a loan."

Gavin seemed to notice for the first time that Stacy was holding his hand. "A regular bank wouldn't have financed this kind of deal. This man isn't a regular banker, Stacy. He's just a man who invests, and he doesn't like to be disappointed."

"Well, we'll just have to see that he isn't. If you'll handle your mother and Aunt Jane, Lonnie and I will repair the car. I promise, I'm very good at what I do."

Maybe the car was her way out too. She had to buy some time so that she could figure out what to do about her father's debt, and she and Lonnie certainly had no other work at the moment. In spite of Gavin's fears, she thought that Lonnie could straighten out the bend in the fender and repaint it to match the rest of the car. But in agreeing, was she solving her problem, or was she binding herself to Gavin Magadan even more?

As conflicting thoughts swept through her mind, he was looking down at her with questioning eyes, eyes that rewrapped her in the fantasy and made her forget her doubts. No matter the reason he'd had for coming into her life, for now they were tied by work, by her job, his future, and that connection was as strong as the physical magnetism that held them.

This time as he leaned over her, she stretched to reach him. His lips melted against hers, and without reservation she answered his desire freely, giving to him the comfort he so desperately needed, that she so desperately needed to give. Hands tightened. Bodies pressed. Tongues danced.

Until the phone rang.

"Saved by the bell," Gavin said as he drew away.

"Bell?"

"The phone, it's ringing. Knowing that my mother and aunt have taken Lonnie hostage, you'd better answer it."

It wasn't Lonnie. It was one of her few remaining regular customers. Greenway's Gravel Company had a truck overheating over on Highway 278. Could Stacy go?

"Sure. No, wait a minute. The wrecker is out right now, and the pick-up . . ." The pickup still had a dead battery. She had intended to recharge it first thing that morning. Before Alice and Jane had come to call.

But Frank Greenway needed her help now. Quickly she made up her mind. "Magadan, how'd you get here?"

"In my mother's Buick."

"Your mother's car? Why didn't they drive it?"

"They did, yesterday. They parked it downtown near their spiritual center and forgot where it was. I just found it this morning."

Stacy thought for a moment, then turned back to the phone. "Got you covered," Stacy told the caller. "I'll be there in ten minutes."

Stacy hung up the phone and began to give orders. "Magadan, take that mat over there and line your mother's trunk. I'll get the necessary tools."

"And what are you going to do, commit murder and hide the body?"

"Not a chance. We're going to repair a dump truck."

Ten minutes later they were pulling behind a truck filled with gravel on the side of the highway.

"What can I do, Stacy?"

Stacy took one look at her driver and shook her head. She couldn't think of a thing Gavin Magadan would be good for, unless they were cruising Neiman-Marcus. Well, she reconsidered, maybe there were a few things. But they couldn't be done on the side of the road in broad daylight.

She crawled under the hood and began to study the situation. She was lucky. Only a broken water hose. She did a quick check on the other hoses and connections and decided that they'd get the driver to the job.

"Okay," she said to Frank's driver as she backed down and wiped her face on her sleeve. "Just sit tight for a few minutes while I take a quick trip to the parts store, and I'll have you moving. Gavin?"

"Of course," he said, opening the car door with the formality of a chauffeur, ignoring the grease she'd wiped on her bottom. It would serve his mother right if her car seat was ruined. It was just dessert for what had happened to his convertible. That wouldn't make them even, but it was a start.

On the drive to the parts store, and later as he listened to Stacy wisecrack with the clerk while he was filling the order for the hose and connections she needed, Gavin took a careful look at the woman who'd become such an integral part of his life.

She was saucy and determined. She was obviously a competent mechanic, and it was obvious that the men with whom she was dealing respected both her work and her as a person. An honest person. A person who worked with her hands and her heart. For he didn't doubt it was her heart that had prompted her to agree to repair his car. Why else would she gather him up and try to comfort him, when he was just as obviously trying to take the thing that made her life important.

All his life Gavin had lived by his wits. Even his job depended not so much on standard business methods—everybody in investments operated the same way—but on his charm and quick wit. He wooed the ladies, drank with the men, played the game with the best of them, until one day he'd grown weary of promising things that he couldn't be sure he could deliver.

It had been Aunt Jane who, after she'd heard someone offer him a fortune for his car, had encouraged his plan to open up a classic car restoration center. Gavin hadn't done the work on his car himself, but he'd managed to locate a crew of workers who had the ability.

Then he'd met an old man, a farmer who through the years had collected what his family considered barns full of junk. To Gavin, the farmer was the answer he'd been looking for, and a partnership became the result. The farmer didn't want to give up his tractors, his cars, and bicycle parts.

That was when Gavin had come up with the idea of building a center to reproduce and restore antique vehicles to be sold, and for private collectors like Gavin who had money without the necessary expertise to restore their cars.

But land around Atlanta had been expensive, and he was getting desperate until his aunt Jane had suggested he look in Paulding County. She'd even suggested Lanham's Garage as a possibility. Long ago, Gavin had stopped questioning his aunt's peculiar storehouse of information. Too often she'd known about things even she couldn't explain. This time she'd been right. The land was selling for a reasonable price, and he could finally envision his future—a future that he initiated and worked for.

But he hadn't counted on Ms. Anastasia Lanham with her attack dogs and her love of horror movies and baseball. He'd never believed that there was a woman on the face of the earth who could understand and accept his family. But then he'd met her. And here he was, assisting a woman with a grease stain across her cheek and a wrench in her back pocket. The Gavin of two days ago would have been working out a plan to force her into selling her business. But the new Gavin was having doubts. Her garage was as important to her as the center was to him.

Gavin watched her lean across the parts counter, watched the way her worn coveralls hugged her bottom, and he felt an answering tug in his lower parts. What was she wearing under her coveralls today? Did those ribbed undershirts and boxer shorts come in assorted colors?

Hell, why was he thinking about her underwear when he was about to be dismembered by a man named Sol the Greek over the destruction of the car. It was as if his body was suffering from a hormone attack that was turning his mind into pure mush. The man who'd advanced him the funds to take options on the land would never understand his inability to force her out and secure the final piece of land. Neither could he.

"Okay, Magadan, let's roll." Stacy was carrying a long cordoned section of black tubing and a small bag of parts. "Now we have to find some water?"

"Water?"

"Yes, we can fix the water hose, but all the water is gone. We'll have to replace it."

"And how do we do that? There don't seem to be many faucets on the side of the road."

"We order take-out."

At this point Gavin didn't argue. He simply followed her instructions to drive to the ice-cream shop nearby, and helped Stacy rinse out and fill six empty gallon syrup jugs. By the time they were finished, Gavin's already stained white Loafers were spotted with raspberry and grape flavoring.

Stacy replaced the hose and filled the radiator with water while Gavin leaned against his mother's car and watched. He was feeling more than a little incompetent as the truck driver held him in a skeptical stare-down. Back at the garage, Stacy filled out her service sheet, figured the bill, and called Larry Greenway to give him the report.

She finished talking to her customer and began shuffling papers around in silence. He felt a strain in the air for the first time since he'd laid eyes on Stacy Lanham.

"Now, then, Magadan," she finally said. "Thanks for your help. But I think you'd better get home and check on the ladies."

"I think what I'd better do is check on Lonnie. With my mother and Aunt Jane, he could be in mortal danger."

"That too." She sat behind her desk, feeling the growing unease. They'd been so caught up in what Stacy was beginning to recognize as a whirlwind of desire that they didn't know how to have a simple conversation. Looking at the man in the linen trousers and the button-down shirt, she was beginning to understand that the differences between them involved more than just life styles. They had nothing in common.

Stacy was into horror movies and books, and she'd be willing to bet that *he* had a copy of *The Hunt for Red October* on his nightstand. She was a baseball nut, and Gavin played tennis. Her stereo, when it played, was stacked with rock and roll. He probably had a CD player and listened to opera. She ate peanut butter sandwiches, and he ate Turkish delights.

But, more than that, he was out to buy her garage, and from what she'd learned, Lucky, and now she, probably owed his aunt Jane more than the garage was worth. It was all such a muddle.

"What?" he asked.

"I don't understand."

"I think you do. You're sitting there analyzing me. I can see you reading my service manual and deciding that I'm a new computer model and you're still into repair the old-fashioned way."

She gasped. How could he possibly know how close he was to what she'd been thinking?

He started around the desk. "That's true, isn't it?"

"No, don't come any closer. I can't think when you're too near. I can't even look at you without forgetting what I'm doing. That's—that's nothing but pure—"

"Lust? Maybe, but how can we be sure? There's something very different about you and me, about how this has all fallen into place. I've never understood how my mother's and my aunt's minds work, but I'm beginning to believe that there is some kind of force working here that we can't turn off."

Stacy refused to look at him. Looking at him

made everything else seem unimportant. She was confused. She'd called herself hexed. He'd called it a force that couldn't be stopped. Never in her life had she been a coward, but to save her life, she couldn't find an answer that would make things what they were before Gavin Magadan had breezed into her garage the previous morning.

"I'm going to send Nick over to help you," Gavin said. "He's the man who'll head up the body shop."

"We don't need any help."

"It isn't a matter of need," Gavin said. "It's a matter of time."

"Are you in that big a rush to get rid of your car?"

"No, before I let it go I'm going to drive it in a parade, a very important parade."

Stacy tried to think. Gavin's mind was more like his aunt Jane's than he realized. What kind of parade was taking place. The Fourth of July had already passed, and it wasn't yet Labor Day. There could be some kind of centennial celebration, but Gavin didn't seem to be the kind of man to go in for that kind of thing, particularly when it would be hard on his car.

"It's a sentimental thing. They're closing Northside, my old high school, in two weeks. The ceremonies start with a parade and end with reunions of the classes who've graduated in the last forty years."

Northside, of course. The exclusive school for those students living on the north side. At least it had started out that way originally. Through the years it had turned into a citywide school for the performing arts, and many wealthy students had switched to private schools.

"I'd have thought you went to one of the private schools like Lovett, or Pace Academy," Stacy said, raising her gaze before she thought.

"You have a lot of wrong thoughts about me, which I intend to change, beginning with my interests. I have tickets to the Braves-Dodgers' game Saturday night. Will you come with me?"

"Tickets for the Dodgers? But I thought they were sold-out."

"I believe they are. Will you come?"

"Will I come? You really want to take me?"

"Of course, who else do I know who can give me a running commentary on the finer points of the game."

"Are you kidding?"

This time he did come around the desk. This time he leaned down and brushed her lips with his lightly, almost as if he were afraid of getting too close. "I never kid a kidder," he said. "I'll send Nick over tomorrow to help Lonnie, and I'll pick you up Friday night about six. Traffic will be pretty bad, and we don't want to miss the first pitch. Who do you like, gambling woman?"

"You want to make a wager?" The air supply in the garage was turning volatile again. Gavin had stepped back, but the oxygen had already over-heated.

"Absolutely," he said with a serious expression on his face. "I'll bet two dollars on the Dodgers. Ah, hell, I mean, ah, shoot, let's get crazy, make it five dollars and dinner."

"You're on, Magadan. You know I can't cook, but you're safe. You also know that I don't lose."

"I know. You only make little bets on sure things."

"That's right. So, if you expect anything more, you're going to be disappointed."

"All I expect you to do, Stacy Lanham, is repair my car and," he grinned as he added, "work on your vamping technique. You're definitely improving, but you still have a way to go."

Lonnie returned after lunch wearing an odd expression of contentment on his face.

"Took you long enough," Stacy commented.

"Well, it turned out that Jane left her keys in the convertible. I had to do a little breaking and entering to get the back door open. Of course Jane explained to the security officer who answered the call that I was only following orders. She's a real special lady, isn't she?"

"Jane? Yes, I suppose she might be called that."

"Yep, you just don't meet many women like her anymore. I think I'll go to lunch now, if that's okay. I thought I'd get myself a haircut."

Lonnie get a haircut? The heavens must have shifted slightly. The charge in the air inside the garage had reached catastrophic proportions and had altered Lonnie's brain waves. "Eh, sure. You can bring me a burger. I'm going to stay here and put the battery charger on the truck."

"By the way, I told Jane and Alice that we'd repair the fender. I'll get started on it first thing in the morning."

"Fine, if you're back to earth by then."

But Lonnie didn't hear her. It was obvious that the music he was hearing came from a different place. Stacy could understand that. She just couldn't believe that her old friend and protector had fallen victim to the same Magadan charm that was jolting her senses.

Stacy made up her mind that she wasn't going to resent Nick. But she was unprepared for his censure when he saw what they had to work with in her garage. She was even less prepared for the delegation of equipment and supplies that arrived with Gavin's friend the next morning.

Where Lonnie was bald and short, Nick was reed slim and bushy. His hair, longer than Stacy's, was actually pulled back in a ponytail that hung down his back. The tattoos on his arms announced that he loved his mother and his car, and once Stacy saw him run his fingers over the crushed fender, she figured out which came first.

Nick's equipment filled all the empty spaces in Stacy's garage as if it belonged there. After a few testy words, the two men started to work, leaving Stacy to deal with any regular calls. By midweek another crew of workers arrived, transforming one work bay into a moisture-proof chamber for painting. Bit by bit, Stacy watched her seedy, run-down facility take on new life, along with the Cadillac.

She hated to admit it, but she spent a great deal of her time watching the doorway, expecting any second to see Gavin striding across the garage. But he couldn't have marched straight through as he'd done that first day. Now the other work bays were filling up. Not with trucks, but with automobiles in need of bodywork. And Stacy was fielding an onslaught of questions about repainting and striping and customizing.

Every time she tried to explain that she ran a fleet garage, Lonnie or Nick stepped in, overriding her refusal with, "If you want to leave it, we'll get to it when we can."

At night she watched *Alien* and identified with Sigourney Weaver, who was being stalked by an unseen enemy. For that was the way Stacy felt. She was alone, in her own house, but still there was a presence, constantly there, reaching out to touch her at moments when she least expected it.

He didn't call, but she heard his voice. He didn't come, but she closed her eyes and saw him as clearly as if he were there.

When Friday night arrived, Stacy had bleached the grease from beneath her fingernails and splurged on two new outfits that were promptly returned in favor of a pair of green shorts and a favorite old "Save the Rain Forest" T-shirt. She did spring for a new pair of white canvas shoes, a three-dollar special from the mart.

Frankenstein and Dracula heard Gavin arrive before she did. When the doorbell rang, they charged through the room in their normal attack mode. At the door they recognized their visitor and sat without being commanded to do so. Stacy lifted her lucky coin to the outside of her shirt and opened the door.

"Would you like to—*come in* was what she started to say, but her words died in her throat as she caught sight of the man who'd marched determinedly through the corridors of her mind all week.

"Oh, yes, I'd like to, very much, but if I come in, I'll kiss you and we'll never get to the game I promised to take you to."

"And you always keep your promises?"

"I always try. How's the car?"

"It's coming along fine. How's the parade?"

They were talking, but the conversation wasn't important. They were standing there with goofy smiles on their faces as if they'd each won a prize on the ringtoss game at the fair.

Damn, the man totally overpowered her. All he had to do was come within two feet of her, and she melted. He was exactly the kind of man she'd sworn she'd avoid. He might not be a gambler, but he was a hustler, and there was little difference between the two. Sure he was gorgeous, with those jewel-green eyes pinning her down as if he were Indiana Jones and she were the treasure he'd been searching for, but she'd already vowed not to fall under his spell.

Of course, he did look after his mother and his aunt. And a man who cared about his family couldn't be all bad. And he was making an effort to build a respectable life with a new career. But that was no reason for her to drift off into la-la land every time he came close.

Then she looked closer. Tonight he even looked different. Tonight he *was* different. Gone were the expensive trousers and the matching tailor-made shirts. Gone were the streaked and speckled white leather Loafers. He was wearing boots and a pair of black jeans so faded that only the seams still showed color, and so tight that they looked as if they'd been painted on his lean, powerful legs. He was wearing a sleeveless ribbed T-shirt and a baseball cap.

"Something wrong? Am I not dressed right for a baseball game?"

Baseball is not the game you're dressed for, she wanted to say. If lust were marketable by the ounce, she'd put him on the scales. If her heart was beating any faster, she'd probably be launched as a receiving satellite and float through space as a transmitter for totally sinful thoughts.

Gatsby was gone. The man she was looking at was all male, and deadly. "You're fine," she finally managed to say. "Are you ready?"

"Oh yes, but first I have one small chore that won't wait." He pushed open the door and swept her into his arms, kissing her soundly before he let out a satisfied sigh and released her.

"Why did you do that, Gavin?"

"I just wanted to be sure that nothing had changed."

"And has it?"

"As my aunt Jane would say, Lordy no! The situation just keeps on keeping on."

Six

"Your chariot, madam. What do you think?"

Gavin asked the question and stopped at the corner of the house by a battered old green pickup truck.

"You're driving this?" Stacy couldn't keep the disbelief from her voice. Gatsby had shed his white linen trousers and tasseled Loafers for skin-tight jeans and boots, but neither image fit with an old, grungy truck.

"Why not? It's a great truck. In fact, I'm going to leave it with Nick and Lonnie. It will be the first restoration job we do."

Leave it with Nick and Lonnie? she repeated to herself. "I don't understand."

"It belongs to one of my partners. He loaned it to me for our date. I thought you would appreciate its potential."

Gavin opened the door and assisted Stacy inside. She wanted to ask why Lonnie was involved in his project. She wanted to ask if he was sure he could drive a straight shift truck. She wanted to ask why he continued to make plans that involved her and her garage in his future. But all she could do was slide across the seat to sit beside him.

"No gun rack on the back window?" she finally asked as he backed smoothly down the drive, maneuvering the old truck beautifully, as if he'd always been behind the wheel.

"Not on this truck. It belonged to the state forestry department once. It's one of the original 1956 models, only three left that we've been able to find. I think it's very appropriate."

"A green forestry truck, appropriate?"

"Sure. It makes me want to climb trees," he said in a wicked, low voice.

"Climb trees?" She was beginning to sound like an echo.

"Your shirt. I definitely want to save it, and the rain forest. It's spectacular. You see what a team we are?"

"What are you trying to do, Magadan? You may drive a Cadillac convertible, but you'll never convince me that you normally drive forestry department trucks. And you certainly don't wear jeans and boots. Where'd you get this outfit?"

"At the thrift shop. Does it show?"

"It shows." She grinned. "It shows everything a man wants to show. Tonight is going to be very interesting."

It was.

Gavin might have been driving a beat-up old truck, but he drove it straight into the VIP parking section. The ticket taker directed them to the front row of seats that was just to the right of the batter's box.

Stacy sat down, glancing directly to her left at the section which belonged to the owner of the

Braves, Ted Turner. "Wow, when you said you wanted to take me out to the ball game, you weren't kidding. How'd you get these tickets anyway?"

"I just called in a few favors," Gavin explained. "Now, about dinner. What would you like?"

"You haven't won the bet yet."

"My stomach doesn't care. It says it's hungry, and my body gets very aggressive if it isn't fed. Besides, just look at this as an appetizer. You can supply the main course after the game."

That's what Stacy was worried about. She had the feeling that *she* was the main course, and the end of the game was still four hours or so away. From the way Gavin was looking at her, she wasn't certain that she wouldn't be burned to a crisp by then.

"Two hot dogs all the way and a lemonade," she said with a gulp.

"Two hot dogs coming up." Gavin signaled to the vender coming down the steps.

Like a small boy, Gavin dived into the food and the game. He was like a two-year-old asking questions. "Why do the players chew tobacco?"

"I have no idea, they just do."

"Why do they wear gloves when they bat?"

"To get a good grip on the wood."

The Braves' pitcher threw the first pitch. The Dodgers' hitter promptly hit it out of the park. The crowd hushed, except for Gavin, who stood and clapped vigorously.

"Gavin! Stop it. You're cheering for the Dodgers, and we're sitting right next to the owner of the Braves."

"Oh, Ted knows. I told him that you were betting on the Braves, and I had a bet on the Dodgers."

"You told Ted Turner you were coming to the game to cheer for the opposition?"

"That's okay. Ted and I go back a ways."

Gavin sat and watched the next three Dodgers make outs, then glanced around at the fans who were rhythmically chopping the air. "What are they doing?"

"That's the tomahawk chop. We're the Braves, remember? It's the fans' way of cheering on the team. They hear the tom-toms and start the tomahawk motion. Have you ever been to a baseball game before?"

"Nope. Have you ever been on the sales floor of a brokerage firm?"

"Nope. Can't say that I have."

"I'll take you."

Stacy wiped a spot of mustard from his nose, meeting his eyes evenly, steeling herself for the answering onslaught of emotion that occurred anytime they looked at each other.

"Gavin," she said, trying to keep her voice calm, "I have as much business in a stock exchange as you do in jeans and boots."

"Why, don't you like the way I look? I was positively assured that this was the appropriate dress for a lean, mean, loving machine who had a date with a vamp."

Loving machine? He had her. Caught like a rabbit in the light of an oncoming automobile, she froze. On both sides of them the fans rose in unison. The tom-toms churned, and the roar of the crowd swirled around them. *Like the way he looked?* Of course she liked the way he looked. Every woman in the stadium liked the way he looked. Every time she moved her head, she encountered the hostile glare of yet another woman staring at Gavin Magadan.

It had always been the same with Lucky. Women had been drawn to him, and he could never say no. He played on that charm, used it to his advantage. It was the women who ended up being hurt, and yet, they never held it against him.

Was that happening to her? Was Gavin turning on the heat in order to influence her? She couldn't be sure. She couldn't even be sure what she was feeling. He totally confused her.

And that was *before* he kissed her.

Right there, on camera, Gavin Magadan had kissed her. When the fans began to make catcalls and whistle, Stacy lifted her head enough to see their picture flashing on the big screen on the opposite field scoreboard.

"Gavin!"

Stacy pulled away, feeling her face flush as she felt every eye in the ballpark on her. Before he realized what she was doing, she was halfway up the steps.

"If you don't want him, honey, I'll take him!" One fan called as she rushed by.

"I'll trade," another shouted.

Stacy was incensed. Every time she met Gavin Magadan, she ended up behaving in some wild, off-the-wall manner. What was happening to her, kissing a man in the ballpark before thirty-five thousand screaming fans? Not to mention the millions more who were probably watching on television.

Lonnie. Lonnie would have seen the kiss. At least he'd have visible confirmation that she'd won that bet. There'd be no question about her having vamped Gavin Magadan. Lonnie would leave her alone about finding a man now. The only question still to be answered was how she could justify what Gavin had done to her.

By the time she left the ballpark, Gavin was striding along behind her. She was grateful for the VIP parking space, otherwise she'd never have found the truck in the sea of vehicles around the stadium.

"All right, so the game wasn't interesting. You didn't have to be shy about leaving." He reached out and caught her arm.

"Don't touch me!"

"What's wrong, Stacy?" He caught her shoulder and swung her around.

"And don't look at me either. You make me crazy when you look at me."

"That's what's supposed to happen. I wouldn't want to be the only one with that problem." Gavin opened the truck door and leaned lazily against the side of the cab.

"What do you mean?"

"I mean the same thing I've been telling you all along. The Force is with us, and we can't fight it. What's wrong with going with the flow. I might get to like baseball."

"I don't know," she admitted. "I just know that sitting in box seats with a man who lives practically next door to the governor's mansion isn't my style. My father traveled in those circles, but I don't."

"So, it's time you did. Why do you keep putting yourself down, Stacy?"

"I don't. I like my life. It's a fine life. You just don't belong in it."

He walked around the truck and got in. "Why not?"

"Because of Aunt Jane."

"I knew it. I didn't know how, but I was sure that Jane had something to do with what was happening. Let's go home and listen to the rest of the game while you tell me. I still have a bet to win."

"No you don't. I told you, I never lose."

"Never say never." He helped her inside the truck and closed the door behind her.

But I don't want you to go home with me, she protested silently as Gavin reached out and pulled her across the seat until their thighs touched. *I don't.*

Gavin turned on the radio. By the time they reached Hiram, it was painfully obvious that Stacy was going to win her bet. With two innings to go, the Braves were six runs ahead and the bases were loaded.

"How come this team is suddenly winning?" Gavin asked curiously. "I mean, I thought the Braves were usually fighting for last place."

"Not this year. They've turned everything around. No more making do with the leftovers."

"Leftovers?"

"Yeah, it used to be that if a player was used up or on his way down, we got him. This year we have new uniforms, new players, and a new confidence. I think the main thing is, if you *think* you're going to win, you stand a better chance. At least that's what Lucky always said."

"And did he?"

"Think he could win? Always. Did he? Rarely."

"How old were you when your father stopped playing ball?"

"I was eight years old."

"What happened then?"

"Lucky and I moved around a lot—until I started

high school. Then Lonnie and I came here. Lonnie's wife, Grace, was still alive then. She died six years ago. Lucky came and went, until I was twenty. He had a heart attack. He died instantly."

"With his boots on, according to Aunt Jane."

"If that means he wasn't alone, yes. He was with—someone. That left just me and Lonnie, and Lucky's debts."

"I can identify with that, all right," Gavin said, as he turned into the gravel drive that led to the log house. "At least so far as my mother is concerned. I never knew my father. My mother and I moved around a lot too. Then later we came here to Atlanta to live with Aunt Jane. But lately it's turning into a question of who's looking after whom."

"Oh, but I thought—"

"You thought I've always had money and position?"

"Yes. You went to Northside. And I've seen your—I mean, Aunt Jane's house."

"Everything I've ever had, Stacy Lanham, I've had to work for. By the time I was in the ninth grade, I was working in the drugstore. I never went to a baseball game because I was always working. Later I went to college a few hours at a time. Until I took a temporary job with Arthur Murray and saw the light. There was more money in dancing than sales. I could keep myself, pay for college, and support my mom."

The drive ended. Gavin parked the truck and turned off the engine.

"You were a dance instructor?"

"The original Dirty Dancer was not Patrick Swayze. It was me." He opened the door and came around for her, taking her by the hand and leading her into the amber light beneath the trees. "Want to do the lambada, baby?"

Maybe he'd gone too far. Or maybe it was sheer nerves. Stacy couldn't help herself, she began to laugh. "Me? Do the lambada? Gavin, I can't do the box step."

"Well, we're going to have to fix that. The reunion is a sock hop, and we're gonna dance."

Gavin pulled her to him, her breast tight against his chest, his left knee pressed intimately between her legs. "Just move with me, darling."

"I knew it," she managed to say as they dipped and swayed across the yard. "Zelda and Scott. All we need is some bathtub gin and a little Charleston music."

"Charleston? You say you want to Charleston?" Gavin changed the tempo and hummed a foxy tune to keep the rhythm of their new step.

By the time they reached the doorway, the dogs were howling and scratching at the screen.

"Gavin Magadan, let me down. I want to find out what's happening in the game."

"The game, dinner, my five-dollar bet." Gavin reached over the door, retrieved the key, and let the dogs inside before releasing his hold on Stacy. "I'll turn on the game. We'll worry about dinner later."

"You worry about dinner. I've already had hot dogs and peanuts and popcorn. The only thing I haven't had is—" She broke off, remembering the only thing left on their menu.

"Dessert," Gavin said. "I remember."

They watched the game. Gavin didn't touch her, other than where their thighs joined as they sat side by side. His not touching her was unnerving.

By the time the game ended, the tension had enveloped her, and she could hardly talk.

"I guess this means you owe me five dollars," she said, her voice sounding strained as she struggled to force air past the painful lump in her throat.

"I guess it does, and dinner and dessert."

"I told you that I wasn't hungry."

"Neither am I—not for food. I want you, Anastasia Lanham, more than I've ever wanted a woman in my life. And I think you feel the same way." He didn't look at her. He didn't move any closer. He didn't take her in his arms. He simply made love to her with his voice.

"Why?" she asked curiously. "I've already learned enough about you to know that you could probably have any woman you choose. Why me?"

He turned so abruptly that she wasn't prepared for the intensity of his gaze, which caught and held her. "I think you must have healing eyes," he said quietly. "There's something wonderfully warm and caring about them. Like fine brandy, like tiger eyes, they comfort and brand me when I look at you."

"I don't understand that kind of talk, Gavin. I never understood when I heard my father talk about abstract feelings and instincts. I only know what I can touch and see and feel. And I don't understand this power that exists between us."

"Neither do I, Stacy. The first time I saw you, I felt good, happy. You were peaches and cream, and I wanted to taste you."

"You doing it again, Gavin, talking about something that can't be touched, or described. Talk to me about reality, about my garage and how you came to be there. About Aunt Jane and why she sent you."

"All right, but I can't do that and look at you." Gavin stood and switched off the television and turned the lamp on its lowest wattage. The room was bathed in soft shadows as he sat beside her and took off his boots.

"I've been working for an investment firm for years. I've done well, but I'm tired of playing games and hustling people—that's what it is, essentially. I try to outcharm my competition, outmaneuver the investor. Times are hard now, and there is just so much money out there. I think that I need some of your reality."

"So you want to buy a garage? Come on, Gatsby, get real."

"No, several years ago I attended an antique car auction and saw perfectly sane men go crazy bidding astronomical amounts of money on the cars they'd always wanted in their youth and could never afford."

"So you're into ego gratification and recapturing youth?"

"That's how it started. But then I had a client who had a huge dairy farm. He and his brother operated it for years. Then progress found them as the city spread out, and eventually the land became worth so much money that he couldn't afford the taxes. When his brother died, he came to me to sell the land for him."

There was something vital and alive about Gavin's voice now. Stacy was glad that he hadn't been able to harness this kind of power into his seduction of her. She would never have been able to resist.

"And?" she prompted.

"Through the years, as the dairy barns had been abandoned, he filled them with things."

"Things?"

"Mostly old things that he cared about. Tractors, farm implements, and automobile parts."

"You mean, he had a junkyard."

Gavin laughed. "Stacy, one's man's junk is another man's treasure. Jim—that's my client—bought up all the old stock in the parts department of every automobile dealership that had changed hands or moved into new buildings. He had two buildings of *new* old car parts. He was sitting on a fortune, and his land was being claimed for nonpayment of taxes."

"And you want to buy my garage to store his car parts?"

"Not exactly. We're going to open a complete center where we'll buy old automobiles and completely restore them to be sold. That, and we'll do private restoration for people who can afford it."

Stacy shook her head. In the half darkness she knew that Gavin couldn't see her. But the concept he envisioned was mind-boggling. And risky. And as grand a scheme as she'd ever heard her father promote in his heyday.

"And you're going to make a million dollars."

"Yes, and probably more. Stacy, I've already taken an option on all the land around yours. I need your garage to complete the project, or the whole deal is down the toilet. I should have come to you first. But I found out that you were practically out of business, and I thought you'd sell in a minute."

She didn't know what she'd expected, but his knowledge of her dire straits came as a surprise. "You had me investigated?"

"Not exactly. Well, yes, my backer did. But that was before I met you, Stacy. Now, well, I don't want to cheat you, and I won't. I simply have to have your land."

"You mean, if you don't get my garage, you lose the project?"

"Something like that. Don't worry, I'll pay you a fair price. You can even come to work for me—you and Lonnie. I've worked with plenty of gamblers in my life, but I don't think I've ever worked with one who never lost."

"You don't have to sweet-talk me, Gavin. You and I both know that you can take my garage if you want to and not pay me a cent. Even your mother and Aunt Jane know that."

Gavin heard the resignation in her voice. He was confused. What did she think he was, some kind of muscle man who would strong-arm her? He wasn't sure where that thought had come from. His mother and Aunt Jane? Of course he was used to their nonsense, but he could see how that might appear to Stacy. Suddenly he understood what she thought.

"Uh-oh, I see. You think I intend to marry you and claim the garage as my wedding present."

"What?" Stacy came to her feet. The dogs joined her instantly, ready to spring to her defense if needed. "Marry you? I never intend to marry, Gavin Magadan, and if I do, it will be to a mailman, or a hardware store owner, or a farmer. In case you don't understand, that means a normal, ordinary man who probably doesn't have a pot to . . . I mean, no money and no grand schemes to make a million dollars."

Gavin stood lazily, took a slow step toward Stacy, and lifted her chin with his thumb, bringing her face into the light spilling from the kitchen beyond.

"Anastasia Lanham, I think we're going to have to take a chance on each other. Grand schemes I may be guilty of, at least that's what the banks said when they turned down my loan applications. But ordinary? If that means that I don't have a pot to do anything in, I qualify. Every cent I have is tied up in this project, along with a hefty sum from a pretty unsavory character from out of town. I'm sorry I'm not a mailman or a farmer, and truthfully, even if I were, I would never feel ordinary when I'm with you."

"Oh." Her voice was breathless.

"And you, my earth child, are no ordinary woman. You pretend to live an ordinary life and yet you're a horror-movie buff, a hobby in which you try to satisfy some wild, secret nature. And you watch baseball, bet on baseball, and live every play vicariously. There is a side of you that you keep hidden very nicely beneath a body that begs to be touched, and I think there is some part of you that wants to break out and live life to the fullest."

Stacy told herself that Aunt Jane was somehow responsible for Gavin coming into her life. And she didn't know why he was saying all these things. She didn't know why she'd brought him home, or gone home with him. She liked her life just as it was. But now, because of Gatsby, nothing was the same.

The dogs whined, then as if on command, turned and left the room. She heard their tags hit the floor as they settled themselves beside the door. Gavin had won their trust, and now her guards were protecting not only her, but him as well. The world would be kept out. They wouldn't move until morning.

Inside her safe haven—the log house where she'd never brought a lover—Gavin Magadan was tearing down every wall she'd ever built. And as she felt his arms curl around her shoulders, she knew that she'd been the one to bring him inside.

"Don't do this, Gavin."

"I think you know that we have to, Stacy."

"But—but I have to tell you. I'm not terribly experienced. It's been a long time since I let a man make love to me."

"Stacy, you're not letting me, and we're not making love—not yet, but we will. And when we do, we'll be loving each other."

As though from a long distance she heard his words, but she was past questioning. A half moan escaped from her lips as she collapsed against him and turned her face to receive the kiss she was becoming dangerously addicted to.

His mouth covered hers in a long, slow kiss that touched off a coil of sensation that bubbled through her veins like hot moonshine in an illegal still. She tried to remind herself that he was out of her reach, that this was some kind of scam, that they were being used or using each other. But nothing could stop the exquisite feelings that had taken control of her practical body and changed her into a wanton woman.

She returned his kiss, delving with her tongue, pressing herself against him shamelessly, seductively. Tonight it wasn't the white-trousered playboy who was wild and mean, tonight it was Stacy who'd turned into a white hot loving machine and who laced her fingers around his neck, holding him until their lungs were filled with fire.

Gavin groaned and pulled back long enough to look down at her. "I have never wanted anyone or anything as much in my life as I want you," he said huskily as he lifted her in his arms and started up the stairs to the loft. At the top of the steps his mouth covered hers in a long, slow, heated assault. The raging fire sweeping through him erupted into a steady, escalating inferno that threatened to burn them both to ashes.

He'd been wrong. It wasn't just warmth and goodness that she promised, it was fire and forever. Through the upstairs window the amber light fell like copper across her bed. He let her down, standing her in the pool of fiery luminance as he began to undress her slowly, being careful not to let his trembling hands betray his anxiety.

When she was standing before him wearing only her bra, he fought the urge to touch her. He expected confusion, reluctance in her eyes. What he saw was a reflection of the fire that must be in his own.

She watched as he pulled his shirt over his head and pitched it over the rail. His boots had already been discarded, now socks followed, and then the jeans, which fell down his legs with more ease than she'd imagined. He, too, stood nearly nude, wearing only his underwear, not a sinful bikini pair as she'd expected, but boxer shorts with—baseballs?

"Oh, Gavin, you crazy, wonderful man." The last residue of doubt in her mind vanished as he flipped the shorts over the balcony and stood aroused and proud—man in his most primeval state, asking woman for her most precious gift.

Gavin was right. Since Lucky died she'd lived

her safe, secure little life, refusing to take risks, refusing the possibility of more loss—until now.

Stacy unhooked her bra and let it fall, allowing her full, aching breasts to hang free. His mouth tightened as his eyes took in the dusky nipples now tightening into rosettes of desire.

She waited until he lifted her once more, knelt, and laid her on the mattress, which was resting directly on the floor. His lips caressed her body, her breasts, down her stomach, scorching the insides of her thigh as he moved slowly toward the coil of heat that seemed drawn into a knot. She felt as if she were about to explode.

"Please, Gavin," she whispered, imploring him with her hands to leave the place he was nipping even as she was pressing herself against him. "Please."

Gavin was drowning in this new emotion; the taste, the touch, the smell of her. He tried to pause, and consider the possible consequence of his action. Anastasia Lanham wasn't some love-'em-and-leave-'em lady, and he wasn't sure any longer that he was a kiss-confuse-and-conquer kind of guy.

Then she reached down and pulled his face up to hers. New waves of desire flared between them as he shivered and melted into the depths of her mouth. Whatever worry had made him pause was pushed aside as he moved his body between her legs. For a long time he simply supported himself on his arms and slid his arousal between her legs, caressing the spot that he'd so inflamed with need. Then he collapsed on top of her, catching his manhood between them, promising her what he was not yet willing to give.

Stacy knew that she must be dying. She felt

every microcosmic particle of her body vibrate in charged readiness. Gavin's face was pressed against her hair, each breath a deep, raspy gasp for air that sounded as if he were drowning. Yet still he waited.

Stacy spread her legs wider, curving them around him, sliding her ankles up and down his legs. And then he raised himself and moved slowly inside her, an inch at a time. If she'd thought she was dying before, she was certain of it now. Nothing in her life had prepared her for this oneness, this blending of one person into another.

Gavin fought for control, tried desperately to hold back the flood of release that was rocking his body even as he entered her. But there was no stopping his climax and as he let it go, he felt the woman beneath him shudder and cry out.

She was flying. She was torn into a million pieces and flying through a field of sensation that she couldn't begin to capture. Then like feathers caught in a hot wind that suddenly died, everything seemed to drift down. Gavin was still inside her, but he was brushing her hair away from her face and kissing her. And for the first time in a long time, Stacy Lanham felt safe.

"Was it—all right?" she asked in a voice that sounded as if it belonged to someone else.

"It was *all* right. It was *all* good. It was spiritual."

Limp and drained, she lay holding him, little sensations still erupting inside her like starbursts of distant summer lightning. Questions still had to be answered, but for now, Stacy felt as if she were soaring, and she was content to wait.

Then Gavin slipped his arm beneath her shoulders and turned over, holding her to him, settling her cheek against his chest. For a long time they simply held each other, allowing the wonder of their loving to settle over them.

Finally she chuckled. "I think, my very special, very ordinary man, that if you really want to make a million dollars, you're in the wrong business. You ought to be a chef."

"A chef? What on earth for?"

"Because if that's your idea of dessert, we can patent it, and we'll never have to worry about anything again."

"Sorry, darling. That's a one-of-a-kind creation. And it's all yours, if you want to claim it."

"Ummm!" Her eyelids were closing in spite of her best efforts to hold them open. She raised her head and found his neck with her lips. "I think I do. Consider yourself immortal, Magadan," she whispered, and gently bit him.

Seven

"You know this doesn't change anything, Gavin."

"I think it changes everything. I've learned my lesson. I'll never bet with you on anything important unless the stakes are higher than ten dollars."

She could smell the male scent of him. Every breath he took made the hair on his chest tickle her cheek. There was a relaxed, content air about him that seemed genuine. He wasn't trying to rouse her to new heights of passion, rather he was wallowing in satisfaction. If she could have seen his face, she was certain he'd be wearing that silly, satisfied smile.

"That's not what I mean, Gatsby. I mean you came, you saw, and you conquered. But it's not going to get you my garage. Now you can pack up and go home."

Conquered? Was that what she thought. He raised up on one elbow and looked down at her. "You think that all this was an attempt to change your mind about selling?" He was stunned, and he wasn't sure whether it was because she was right or because she was wrong.

The garage had brought them together, and he couldn't deny that it was important, but Stacy had touched him in a way he couldn't even begin to describe. What he was feeling was too new and too special to put into words without sounding like the user she'd assumed him to be.

"Of course," she answered honestly, without malice. "You're not the first playboy I've known, nor the first one to use charm and sex to get something he wanted from a woman. You can't help it. I understand, I truly do."

His arm tightened protectively about her. She was wrong, but denying it wouldn't convince her. No, he had to overcome her past by bringing it out into the open so that he could fight whatever dragons she feared.

"Tell me about it, Princess. Who hurt you so badly that you've hidden yourself away from the world in coveralls and a garage?"

"Don't call me that!"

"Princess? Why not? You have a very royal name, Anastasia. You should be wearing diamonds and ermine."

"I'm not tall enough to be royal," she protested, trying to turn the intensity of the moment into a joke.

She retreated into her quick wit, not yet ready to be honest with him. Gavin considered pushing, but decided that he would be better off waiting. Instead, he matched her jovial banter with his own.

"Neither is Queen Elizabeth, but she is. Belonging to royalty is something you're born with, something inside, not how you look. And you, my darling, are positively noble, except maybe when you let out those little screams of pleasure when you're loving me."

"I wasn't loving you. We were simply—I mean, I do not scream in pleasure."

"Oh, yes you do, Princess, and I want to know why you're so afraid to know it." He pressed his lips to her forehead, kissing each eyelid, making hot little circles as he waited. "Tell me about him—the playboy. I want to know, Stacy. I want—no need to know all about you."

And suddenly she wanted him to know. In a great wave of relief she told him the truth, knowing that her past would likely send him away and bring this miracle fantasy to an end. If she wasn't noble enough for this man, she needed to know now, before she fell any further under his spell.

"Not him," she said softly, "them. There was a time, just before my father died, when Lucky got very scared. Nothing was going right for him. He'd always left me behind with Lonnie and his wife, Grace. But suddenly Lucky decided that he needed a talisman. I was that charm. He dressed me up, took me with him, paraded me before all the men he was trying to impress. I never understood why."

"I can almost understand that, Stacy. There's a goodness, an honesty about you that makes a man feel confident, like royalty. You can't see it, but you know it's there."

"I was only twenty, too young to understand that it was all a game. When the men took Lucky into their circles, Lucky took me. From Monaco to Saint Moritz, we traveled with all the rich and famous. I thought they were wonderful, wearing their tuxes and Rolex watches, driving their sports cars and spending money like it was nothing. For a time Lucky was on top of the world, and so was I."

"What happened?"

"One night there was a high-stakes poker game. Lucky won for most of the evening, then after midnight, he started to lose. Finally he was down to his last silver dollar, and he had a winning hand. He didn't have anything else to bet. Well, Sol, the man he was playing with, made a suggestion of what he'd accept for Lucky to call the bet."

Sol? Gavin couldn't decide whether it was he or Stacy who'd stiffened. He knew that name. He knew it well. Sol was the man who'd loaned Gavin the land option money, the man who wanted the car. But Sol and Stacy? In the copper light he saw her eyes closed tightly, and he knew.

"Lucky bet you?"

"No, he didn't. He gave me the silver dollar, folded, and lost. But he thought about it, and in that moment I understood. Even in winning, Lucky lost. They all lost because they'd lost touch with honor and what was important. I came home to the cabin, to Lonnie and Grace. I never left again. Two weeks later, Lucky died—in bed with Sol's daughter.

Gavin was stunned. He hadn't known about Lucky's connection to Sol. Sol, the Greek shipping magnate who had his fingers in every kind of finance worldwide, wasn't a crook. He didn't have to be. He had enough money to pick his financial ventures, and the clout to follow through. But Gavin knew his reputation for eventually taking over every project in which he invested.

Gavin had handled transactions for Sol in the past, so it hadn't been a complete surprise when he'd called about some new proposition. Still, when the conversation worked itself around to Gavin's plan, and Sol had ended up agreeing to put up money for Gavin's project, it had come as a surprise. And it had turned out to be his only option.

But Stacy? Could Sol have known about Stacy? If so, Gavin had put her at risk. And she was worrying about her past association with a group of playboys.

"Ah, Stacy, darling. You're not like them. Believe me, I know. You never went along with that kind of life. You're too gentle and caring."

"Oh no? Let me show you."

She slid from the bed and opened the sliding doors to her closet, switching on the inside light. Hanging there were satin dinner gowns, designer dresses, boxes and boxes of matching shoes, and other clothing that Gavin had seen in the closets of other women in his past.

"I went along with what Lucky expected of me, for a while. Went along and loved it—the glamour, the excitement. Until I saw what it could do. That's why I work in a garage, Gavin. Why I don't bet more than ten dollars, why I won't sell my garage, and why I can't let myself believe anything you promise. Because, until that night, I loved the life. I really did."

"But, Princess, I'm not your father. I'd never do anything to hurt you."

"No, but you're like him, Gavin Magadan, and I'm scared to death of falling in love, scared to death I am falling in love with you." She dropped to her knees and looked at him, wide-eyed and still. "Don't you see? I can't take a chance on going through that again. And you can't promise me that I won't have to."

Gavin stood, walked over, and dropped to his knees in front of her. She was right. He couldn't promise that he wasn't like her father. He couldn't promise she wouldn't be hurt. He was a kind of gambler, and this time the gamble was personal. He'd gone out on a limb, trusting that he could accomplish his goal. But the truth was, he couldn't find a banker willing to finance the project. Sol would back him all the way, but he knew too well that Sol's money came with a price tag. And he was afraid that price might be revenge. He'd used Sol's advance as option money on the land and now he either had to repay it, or he'd have to let Sol in on the deal. Now, more than ever, that option was impos-- sible. This was the nineties, and he felt as if he were a gangster in some forties Humphrey Bogart movie.

Because Stacy was right about one thing. He was pretty sure they were falling in love.

"Maybe you should be worried," he said. "Maybe I can't promise you that you won't be hurt. But that doesn't change the way I feel. It doesn't change the magic that brings us together. Tell me, darling, how do we make this go away?"

All he did was touch her face, and she was in his arms again.

"Oh, Gatsby."

"Once more," he whispered his desperate plea, "let me love you once more, then I'll go. I'll find a way out of this mess, I promise."

And then he remembered the nagging thought that had made him pause before. "Stacy, are you—I mean, I should have asked before, is it all right for me to love you?"

"All right?" Stacy repeated his words, still caught up in the wonder of his touch. "All right? It's more than all right," she whispered. "I think you know that."

This time, when they made love it was slow and sweet, without spoken commitment, without promises. There was just the physical commitment of two people who needed each other and the warmth and promise that came with the loving.

For the rest of the night Gavin held Stacy in his arms. He felt washed in the wonder of what they'd shared, what they'd given to each other. He couldn't explain the contentment she brought to him. It was as if he'd been running toward it all his life and had not known what he was seeking, until that first moment their gazes had connected. The connection had stayed strong, drawing them together.

He understood her fears, how she was torn between loving her father and fearing his need to be somebody. He ought to, for he'd shared that kind of fear and need.

Frightened at the depth of his feelings, Gavin tightened his arm around her, pulling her higher on his body so that she was no longer touching the bed. As his hand stole across her body and clasped her breast, his lips sought her cheek.

Her face was wet.

"Princess, are you crying?"

"No. Yes. I guess I am."

"Why, did I hurt you? I know that I rushed things. I couldn't seem to stop myself. I'm so sorry."

"Oh, Gatsby, darling. I'm not crying because I'm hurt. I'm crying because I'm happy. I'm scared. I'm feeling so many things I can't describe."

Her fingertips ranged across his chest, finding their way through the swirls of hair.

"If you feel any lower," he said in a raspy voice, "you're going to have a man in extreme agony."

She did.

He was.

"Whatever you've been feeling, Stacy, I promise you that it is nothing in comparison to me. Tell me. Don't hide it. I sure can't."

"What I'm feeling feels good, Gavin. It's . . . it's awesome." She propped herself on one elbow and encircled him with a velvet glove of warmth. Her lips danced across his face, touching every part of him with fire as she explored him greedily, with both her fingertips and her mouth.

If Gavin had thought himself balanced on the brink of an implosion before, he was within seconds of self-destruction now as he caught her with his hands and lifted her in the air.

"What are you doing, Gavin?"

"I'm about to give myself to you, darling, in every way I can."

He lifted her forward, catching his probing head in the heated flesh of her body, and letting her slide slowly down. But she wasn't content to be still and slow. Above him she rocked and jerked. He caught her hips and held her still, trying desperately to slow the inevitable explosion. But it was useless. Gavin clenched his teeth, his fingertips digging into her soft flesh as he felt the avalanche of trembling that had already begun.

Stacy cried out, leaned back, and let out a little scream. This time she heard herself, her wanton yelps of desire. But she couldn't stop. And then he was rolling her over and taking control, plunging deeper and deeper as he felt the starbursts and rockets go off, taking them to the fiery brink and singing their bodies with cosmic dust.

It was almost morning when he stole downstairs and dressed. Then he climbed the steps again and stood in the doorway, gathering the image of her lying tousled in the bed covers, storing it forever in his memory.

"Don't worry, Princess, I won't hurt you. I don't know how I'll work this out, but I will."

She didn't answer. She knew there were no answers.

"I have to be away next week, but I'll be back for you and the convertible Saturday morning, early."

"Why?"

"We're going to a parade, remember? And bring your best high school sock hop dancing clothes. We're going to close a school—in style."

He wasn't taking her fears seriously. She'd told him about Lucky and how she felt about being associated with a high roller, and he wasn't listening. Though she knew that Lucky had loved her, his need to gamble had been stronger. For the first time she understood, because the same kind of need was keeping her from letting Gavin go. She'd already begun to sing with the music of excitement simply because he'd become a part of her, and she knew they had to play out the hand.

"'Night, darling," he whispered. "Think of me while I'm away."

He turned to leave.

"Gavin?"

In a heartbeat he was back at her bedside. "Yes?"

"You don't need those clothes."

"I don't?"

"Anybody can wear bad boy clothes. It takes a real lean, mean, loving machine to wear boxer shorts with baseballs."

The next day, almost in a dream, Stacy relived every moment of the time she and Gavin had spent together. Only when she repeated his question aloud –"Is it all right?"—did his meaning wash over her. He'd been asking if she was protected, and she'd thought he was asking permission. She'd assured him that everything was fine. It wasn't. But after a quick trip to a doctor nearby, she made her answer a reality.

The next week passed in a fog. Nick and Lonnie finished the convertible and started on the other work that had filled the garage. The mysterious partner, Jim, appeared, wearing overalls and a wide grin. He wasn't a high roller. He was just a man like Lonnie and Nick, and he began moving dusty yellow and blue boxes of car parts into the parts room. The phone kept Stacy busy, and she tried very hard not to dwell on the impossibility of a future with Gavin Magadan.

Always before she'd been able to look at her life logically, even while she was playing at being her father's gambling partner. She'd known that they were traveling down a road that was an illusion, but once there, she'd allowed herself to become addicted to it for a while. But Lucky could never see past the next scheme that was sure to recoup all his losses. And little by little she'd watched him sell everything he'd accumulated over the years.

Now all she had left was the garage, and slowly but surely, it was being filled with antique cars by a man who'd touched her life with fire and vanished, leaving behind a bank of smoldering coals.

She didn't know what to do with the money she was making on the new rush of work being done by Nick and Lonnie. She made very careful records and deposited the money in a new account she'd opened under the name Lanham Classics. The name was a futile attempt to preserve a business that seemed less and less hers.

Alice and Aunt Jane didn't come to the garage again, but several times Stacy heard Lonnie talking on the phone in a low, teasing voice that was a dead giveaway to the fact that he was talking to a woman. Lonnie hadn't shown any real interest in a woman since Grace had died six years earlier—until now.

"Jane again?" she'd asked once.

"Eh, yes. She's very interested in the work we're doing here."

"And in the man doing it, too, I gather."

"Well, it is nice to have someone your own age who thinks you're fascinating, isn't it, Stacy?"

"What do you mean?"

"Look, kiddo, I may be old enough to be your father, but I'm not dead yet. I can feel the thermal waves when Gavin comes around. You can't fool me. You're interested in the guy, and he's interested in you."

"Maybe, but, Lonnie, that's all it can ever be."

"Why? I've been telling you for years to remember you're a woman and find yourself a real man."

"I know. Your matchmaking is what got us into this mess. Remember?"

"You were the one who took him home, not me."

"I know, and that's what's driving me bonkers. Lonnie, what am I going to do?"

"For once I think Lucky might have been right about taking a chance. Go for it."

"But what if I get hurt?"

"What if you do? Suppose you don't? Think about the stakes."

"I have. I am. And I think they're too high. If you or Nick hear from Gavin, I think I'd better talk to him. I'm not going to that parade with him. He'll have to find someone else."

"Uh-huh, sure. I'll tell him."

But on Saturday morning Stacy was standing in her closet, staring at the clothes she hadn't worn in years. She'd graduated from high school in the early eighties, the boring generation that had offered nothing new or avant garde. She'd never thought that she'd wear any of the clothes Lucky had bought her again, but she found herself choosing a soft purple designer dress with matching shoes. Inside a clutch purse she placed fresh makeup, comb, and cologne.

She never acknowledged that she was getting ready for Gavin as she styled her hair with hot rollers and applied eye shadow and lipstick, but she was. She didn't admit that she had thought about little else during the past week, but she hadn't. She refused to give in to the tingle of response that was already glowing inside her.

Finally dressed, she studied herself in the mirror. The woman she saw was nothing like the woman who wore coveralls every day. She was, she acknowledged, nothing like the woman who'd worn these clothes eight years before either. That Stacy had been wide-eyed and awestruck, and except for a few awkward moments in high school, totally innocent. The eyes she saw reflected in the mirror had known real passion, and her cheeks flushed at the memory.

And then Gavin was there, ringing the doorbell. Stacy took a deep breath and opened it, waiting apprehensively for his reaction.

"Lordy, Aunt Jane told me to expect an angel," he said, letting out a long, ragged breath. "If I weren't afraid of being struck by lightning, I would question her sources."

Stacy could have told him about lightning. She felt as if she'd already been struck. Gavin was wearing his Valley Road clothes, more white trousers and a new pair of white Loafers. But this time he'd matched them with a red-knit shirt that was the same color as his car.

"You're beautiful," they both said in unison.

"I've missed you," was the copycat response.

"Do you think I'd ruin your lips if I kissed you?" Gavin asked, still standing in the doorway.

"I think they might pucker up and die if you don't."

He did.

And she knew that for one day, one morning, in the bright summer sun, she wouldn't think about anything except this loving man and the joy he brought into her life.

The parade participants met in the parking lot of the mall nearest the school. Antique cars representing all the years lined up behind the current Northside Marching Band and waited. On the door of Gavin's car hung a white felt sign with a purple tiger and his year of graduation in large purple letters.

Purple and white balloons were tied to every

antenna, and a number of ambitious participants had managed to stuff themselves into their original cheerleading and athletic uniforms. From the senator riding in the lead car, to the three freshmen pulling a man-size blown-up tiger in a large red wagon in the rear, the mood of the crowd was very festive.

Stacy looked around. There were Model T's, sports cars, limos, station wagons, a pickup truck, and even a purple hearse with aged students carrying signs reading "To Hell With North Fulton," their ancient sports rival.

Everybody who walked by looked at Gavin curiously, and a few of them gathered in small gossipy groups. Stacy was beginning to wonder if any of Gavin's friends had returned for the special celebration when the siren on the police car signaled the beginning of the parade, and the slow moving line of vehicles snaked its way down Peachtree and through the neighborhood to the campus of the school that was being closed.

Along the route cameras and camcorders recorded the event. Newspaper and television reporters met the group in the school parking lot, zeroing in on the senator and the hearse. The event organizer, a sleek blonde wearing a designer outfit, was pointing out special VIPs to the media when Stacy realized from the gestures that the woman in charge was being asked about Gavin. But she was shaking her head and giving a beats-me expression.

"I think you're about to make the six o'clock news, Gatsby," Stacy said as the photographers moved toward them.

"Great. It'll be good publicity for Magadan Classics."

"And you, sir?" One of the camera carriers asked, "Are you a graduate of Northside?"

"Class of 1980," Gavin said with what amounted almost to a dare in his voice.

"What kind of car is this?" someone asked.

"A 1952 Cadillac convertible, restored by Magadan Classics."

"I don't believe I know you," the blonde said, studying Gavin.

"You probably don't. The name is Gavin Magadan."

"Were you involved in the School of Performing Arts?" one reporter asked.

"Nope."

"Sports?" another inquired.

"Nope."

"But you do look familiar," the blonde remarked, her expression growing even more perplexed as she took in the man who looked every ounce of his aunt Jane's Valley Road success.

"Yep. I made deliveries to your house, Michelle. I worked at the Travis Drugstore on Howell Mill Road. I even asked you for a date once."

Michelle's face blanched as she remembered.

"And this," he turned back to Stacy and pulled her close, "this is my lady, Anastasia Lanham, of the royal Lanhams. She is the sole owner of Lanham Trucking Company and Fleet Garage. Shall we go in, darling? I want to show you the window I once jumped out of during biology class."

The clicks of the cameras recorded Stacy and Gavin's regal exit, and the media people trailed after them into the building.

"Why did you do that?" Stacy whispered furiously.

"Sorry, the devil made me do it. I would never have thought of it if Michelle hadn't been standing there looking so smug. That's just the way she looked in high school when I asked her for a date, just before she started to laugh."

"She turned you down?"

"Not exactly. It was all right for me to kiss her in the bushes, but she couldn't be seen with me in public. I wasn't in her class back then."

Like me, Stacy wanted to say. But one look at Gavin's face as he relived all the old painful memories made her keep quiet.

"Was I in the School of Performing Arts?" he mimicked. "I was too busy trying to pay for my clothes and save enough money for college, and bailing my mother or Aunt Jane out of some scrape or another until the next dividend check came in. It's very hard to run with the wealthy and be poor."

"I know about that. Do you think they can look at us now and tell?"

They'd reached what used to be the school cafeteria. In the glass windows overlooking an area with trees and benches, Gavin stopped. "Look at the reflection of those two people in the glass. Do they have status signs around their necks?"

"No."

"It's obvious that they are royalty, and they look absolutely great together."

Stacy heard the sudden relaxation in his voice, and she understood. He'd never been to a baseball game. He'd never had time for normal high school activities. He'd been the outsider once, but no longer. Gavin had come back to his past with both feet planted firmly on top of the mountain. For today he could bask in his success. The question was where would he go from there.

Stacy looked at them in the glass and pushed aside her reservations. This was his moment, and he'd chosen to share it with her. She wouldn't spoil it for him. She'd give him time at the top to survey his choices. Underneath they were not so very different. They just had to decide whether he was coming down or whether she was going to try to climb back up again.

"Gavin, old man!" A huge man with the biggest feet Stacy had ever seen caught Gavin in a bear hug. "How's it hanging?"

"Alvin, good to see you. Let me introduce you to Stacy, my girl."

"Oops, sorry, ma'am. I apologize for my loose talk, but I never did learn my social graces."

Alvin wasn't Gavin's only friend. Stacy met several, all of whom recounted stories of Gavin's friendship and hard work. The rest of the day was a blur of reminiscences, speeches, and official ceremonies. The school cafeteria cranked out a typical lunch, over which a typical food fight broke out, with the instigators being sent to the principal's office by two elderly teachers who'd come back for the closing of the school.

There were tears, awkward moments, and silly giggles, and through it all Stacy began to see Gavin as the rich boy with the family but not the funds. He'd had to work twice as hard as the truly impoverished, because his mother and his aunt had had to be protected. Stacy knew that neither woman ever understood what Gavin had to go through. But she did, and her heart hurt for him.

Lucky had wanted to play ball and he had, but his gift had been taken from him and he'd tried to recapture the glory through tricks and sham. Gavin's glory had been there from birth, but he'd had to hustle to hang on to it, not for himself, but for his family. Stacy could understand both men, and she could love them both.

Later, at the dance, Gavin looked around with satisfaction. He'd made it. His success had never been a secret. He'd done business with most of the men in the area, belonged to their clubs, traveled in their circles. But until now, it hadn't seemed real. He caught sight of Stacy, beautiful, warm Stacy, in her simple purple dress, dancing with the great-great-grandson of Atlanta's famous newspaper editor, Henry Grady.

"Hi, Gav, want to find some bushes?"

Michelle was standing beside him, her lips parted in a sexy pout.

"I don't neck in the bushes anymore, Michelle."

"No? Too bad. There are a couple outside the cafeteria that look just about right. You look good, Gavin. Why haven't we crossed paths since you became king of the mountain?"

"I don't get to either Europe or Hilton Head much. I understand that's where you live."

"My husband's into tennis and wine. What interests you now, other than the daughter of a gambler?"

"You know Stacy?"

"No. I knew her father, or I knew of him. He had quite a reputation with the ladies. Lucky Lanham was supposed to be very special in bed. What about you, Gavin? We never tried a bed."

He gave serious consideration to her question, never allowing his eyes to lose sight of Stacy. "I'd say yes to your observation, Michelle, but not to your invitation. You're a lot of years too late. Now, if you'll excuse me, I want to claim my lady. We have to get back to Frankenstein and Dracula. It isn't safe to leave them alone after midnight."

Over her partner's shoulder Stacy watched the exchange between Gavin and Michelle. She saw the shock on Michelle's face when Gavin walked away, and felt the familiar warmth flood through her when his gaze met hers. When Gavin touched Henry's shoulder, he released Stacy, and she turned naturally into Gavin's arms, settling there in a comfortable togetherness. She was complete again.

"I've missed you, Princess," he whispered in her hair.

"Why didn't you claim me?"

"I did. I have—now." And he pulled her so close that she could barely breathe. "Oh, lady, can we get out of here?"

"It's your party, Gavin. I'm ready when you are."

And she knew instantly that he was ready too. The evidence of his readiness was pressing insistently against her, and she was quivering in response.

"You know I heard talk about this kind of thing happening to a guy on a dance floor," he said.

"Don't tell me you never went to a dance either?"

"Oh, I went, but I never danced. Too shy and too horny. I got this way just watching the women."

"This way? You mean, you stood in the shadows and—"

"Now, I didn't say that. I found a way to be with the ladies, or rather they found a way—outside in the dark, where their dates didn't know. The secret stud of Northside High, that was me. Deliver your order and a little something extra. The store manager loved me—not literally, you understand."

"You mean, you made love to those women, but you didn't date them and you didn't dance with them?"

"It wasn't love, Stacy," he said, waiting until the circling light overhead moved on, leaving them in the shadows so that he could cup her bottom and pull her wickedly against his erection. "Not like this. This is the first time I've ever—"

But he never finished his sentence, for she caught his face and pulled his lips down to meet hers. For the second time since she'd known him, they'd shared a public kiss, a hot, deep, passionate kiss with a part of the world looking on.

"Take me home, Gavin," she finally said, "and dance with me. I want you to love me. All night long."

Eight

They did make love. In the darkness, up the stairs, removing pieces of clothing as they kissed. In Gavin's arms, Stacy forgot all her questions and all her doubts. She wouldn't ask questions. She would take what life offered without worrying about the consequences.

She was weak. She acknowledged that fact at the top of the stairs as Gavin removed her dress. Even if he was only temporary in her life, he was real and she wanted him. They clung to each other in the silence, both mute, both caught up in the wonder of their feelings.

"Are you mine?" Gavin whispered as he lay her down on the bed.

"Yes," she said. *For now,* she added silently. *Until you get what you want and move on.*

Gavin didn't question her answer. He'd always flown by the seat of his pants, taking whatever came and turning it to his advantage. But he'd never expected when he'd walked into Lanham's Garage that he'd discover a rainbow. Only Aunt

Jane believed in leprechauns and pots of gold, and she'd sent him to Stacy.

And every minute since, he'd found his attention focused on Stacy. He'd reached out for Stacy, to touch her, to feel the surge of confidence that her touch inspired. And he'd shared his past and his fears. Then, suddenly, he wasn't on the outside anymore. The people he'd always emulated were no longer important. They were just people. Stacy, in her quiet way, had reached inside that cold spot of uncertainty and filled it with confident warmth. And he was falling in love for the first time in his life.

Gavin lay there in the darkness, smiling. When he left her, just before sunup, he felt as if he were leaving a part of himself behind.

When Stacy awoke, there was a note on the pillow.

"I'll be back. Keep the home fires burning."

Stacy spent Sunday morning lazing in bed, the dogs on either side of her watching her curiously. Staying in bed was new to them, but their expressions said, hey, they could learn to like it if Stacy did. Stacy knew that she was living on borrowed time. Nothing was settled. Nothing had even been discussed. Every time she started to talk about the garage Gavin kissed her and every rational thought vanished.

In the light of morning, the question of Aunt Jane lingered in Stacy's mind. Gavin didn't seem to attach any importance to Jane's connection to Lucky. He accepted the fact that his aunt had some kind of special sixth sense and didn't question it. But Stacy had heard the exchange between Alice and Jane about Lucky. She knew that Lucky had taken Jane's money and, according to Lonnie, never repaid it.

Trying to make sense of Gavin's buying her garage when Aunt Jane might even have grounds for claiming it in lieu of debt was simply not possible. When she'd asked Lonnie, he'd told her for once in her life to leave it alone. Stacy couldn't do that forever. But for now, when the doorbell rang and the boys dashed downstairs wagging their stumpy tails, she knew that Gavin was back. When she opened the door and found him there with her favorite cheese-and-tomato pizza, every worrisome thought fled.

Sunday afternoon they ate pizza and watched the Dodgers take the last game of the Braves' three-game series. For dinner Gavin broiled steaks to perfection while Stacy made a credible salad and heated rolls in the microwave.

Dessert, the nonfattening and sinfully lush enjoy-in-bed kind, quickly became a welcome, familiar treat that extended into the dark hours after midnight. The new Dean Koontz book lay on Stacy's nightstand half-finished as it had for days. She'd read hundreds of books in her lifetime, but there was only one Gavin. And he filled her mind so completely that there was no room for anything else.

Monday morning things were back to normal, or as normal as work could be in a garage that was already filling with special orders for antique vehicles. Stacy had never realized that so much work existed, that so many cars existed to be restored, that so many people would pay to have the work done. With Jim and his brother Stash came an accountant who was prepared to set up a proper bookkeeping system. He had Magadan Classics checks and a computer.

"But the business belongs to me," Stacy said firmly. "And any check written will be written by Lanham Classics."

"Fine," the accountant agreed. "Mr. Magadan said for me to set up the system so that it can be easily converted when the time comes, but we're to use your account and you'll sign the checks and vouchers in the meantime."

"Mr. Magadan doesn't have the authority to *say* anything," Stacy protested hotly. *Just because he's spent the weekend in my bed doesn't mean he owns me.* This was her business, or was it? She didn't know anything anymore.

After an hour of pacing back and forth trying to make sense of her situation, she decided that the only thing to do was stop holding back and get to the person who could settle the issue—Aunt Jane.

"I'm going out for a while," Stacy said to the men who nodded and kept on with what they were doing. She stood at the doorway and scanned the busy scene. Everything had changed. Lonnie had finally found a way to keep her fingernails out of the grease. She felt a little pang of martyrdom. She should be happy with what was happening, but she only felt left out and confused.

All the more reason for getting the issue settled, she decided, leaving the accountant accounting, and the mechanics mechanicking at ten-thirty on a Monday morning. She took the pickup because it was the only mode of transportation she had—except for the wrecker. Lonnie might drive that battered machine up the Valley Road drive, but she couldn't.

Stacy held her breath until she determined that Gavin's car wasn't in the garage. She stopped in the courtyard and waited for the kitchen door to open and the two women to come noisily out to greet her.

"Anastasia, you must have known we needed you," Jane said with a satisfied nod of her head, as she opened the door to the truck and climbed inside.

"We're so glad to see you," Alice added, crawling into the truck beside Jane and slamming the door.

Jane arranged her purse in her lap. "Let's go. We didn't know where we'd find a truck but the cards said one would come."

"We're so glad, Anastasia, that it's you. Jane knew that you'd approve."

As always, the whirlwind surrounded them, and before Stacy knew what was happening, they were driving down Peachtree Street to one of Atlanta's biggest churches.

"Why are we going to church on Monday morning?" Stacy asked.

"To pick up the cots, Anastasia."

"And then we have to stop by the Georgia Power Company and talk to Randall. You did call the club, didn't you, Alice?"

"Of course, Jane. We're taking Randall to lunch," Alice explained. "Of course he'll end up taking us. He always does. We wouldn't want to hurt his feelings . . . he's such a gentleman."

In the midst of the rapid exchange of conversation, Stacy was able to figure out that Gavin had disabled their car in order to keep them at home while he was out of town. Stacy felt something she couldn't identify at the knowledge that Gavin was out of town and hadn't told her. But she had no right to feel anything, she told herself. After all, they weren't engaged or committed or anything, were they?

The deacon at the church explained that they were closing out their shelter for the homeless and were more than willing to make the cots they'd been using available to Jane and Alice for their center. In fact, the minister was lending them one of his volunteers who had already contacted the restaurants in downtown Atlanta and arranged for their excess food to be delivered to the downtown center.

"Yes indeed," Jane explained happily, "the Lord helps those who help themselves. He's already sent us beds, food, and a shelter director."

It was over chicken salad at the club that Stacy learned the reason for the lunch with Randall.

"Now, Randall," Alice was saying, "we don't expect the power company to give us free power indefinitely, just until Gavin is able to arrange corporate donations to take care of expenses."

Stacy simply sat back and watched the two women work. By the time they ordered and polished off dessert, the CEO of the power company had agreed to provide three months' free power to the Shelter for the Spiritual Odyssey of Man, and women, too, Alice added proudly.

It was over midafternoon tea that Stacy finally had the opportunity to ask Jane about Lucky.

"Aunt Jane, I don't know how to ask you this, but I have to know."

"Know what, Stacy? About Lucky and me? I've been waiting for you to ask. I'll tell you anything you want to know."

"Did he take your money?"

"Take my money? Lordy no. I gave it to him. I considered it an even exchange. If I'd had more, he could have had that too."

"But didn't you invest in his ice-skating rink?"

"Of course not, I invested in Lucky. I bought three months of pure lust. It wasn't his fault I didn't have a child. I was already too old, I guess. But I loved every minute of it. Lucky never lied about what he was offering, and I never lied about what I was asking. You know your father, whatever he did, he went all out for it."

"You mean, you just wanted—a child?"

"Oh, no. Not just a child—Lucky's child. I knew at the time it was a wild shot, but hey, nothing ventured, nothing gained. And the venture was pure heaven."

"But didn't you expect him to marry you?"

"Of course not. But I would have been willing."

"But Alice said that he didn't show up for the wedding."

"That's true. In a weak moment we committed ourselves. In the end, I had to confess it was my fault that the wedding didn't take place. At least I like to tell myself that it was."

Stacy's head was spinning. She thought that Lucky's head probably had spun, too, if it was Jane who'd stopped the wedding. "Why did you stop it?"

"Lucky thought I was wealthy. I wasn't. The money I gave him was all I had. I couldn't let him marry me under false pretenses. That would have been dishonest. Lucky never misled me. He only wanted a wealthy wife to be a mother to his daughter. That would have solved both our needs, but it would have been unfair. I did the only thing I could do."

"She burned the skating rink down," Alice said, speaking for the first time during the exchange between Jane and Stacy.

"*You* burned it down, Aunt Jane?"

"That I did. Of course I didn't think that the cops would discover it was arson. I thought that Lucky would collect on the insurance, and he'd have all the money he needed, and it wouldn't matter if I was penniless."

"What happened," Alice went on to explain, "was that he was the prime suspect, and he ended up losing everything."

"Of course I had to let him go then. He thought I'd changed my mind. But I never lost touch with him. I even knew about you and your little garage. And when Gavin started talking about land and a restoration center, I knew I had the chance to make it up to Lucky for what I'd done."

Stacy was stunned. She couldn't believe the astonishing story she'd just heard. At the same time she knew that Jane and Alice were telling the truth. Here she'd been worrying that Jane was trying to take her garage and she was trying to do just the opposite. Sitting there with her red hair hanging in errant tendrils, wearing a miniskirt and go-go boots, was the woman who might have been her stepmother if an ice-skating rink hadn't burned fifteen years ago.

"I'm very sorry, Stacy," Jane said. "I never wanted you to know. But when Gavin brought you home, I understood the master plan. Your aura so perfectly matched his, there was no dividing them."

"Why yes," Alice added, "we've even unearthed Jane's wedding dress, the one she bought to marry Lucky in. We think it will fit you beautifully."

"But, I'm not going to marry Gavin," Stacy protested. "I can't live on Valley Road. I don't even want to."

"Don't worry, you won't have to. I'm going to sell the house and give the money to Gavin so he can repay that awful Sol. He thinks that he'll be able to talk Sol into backing out of their deal, but he won't. Sol will try to take over, that's the way he operates. And Gavin won't be able to stop him."

"Gavin's gone to talk to Sol?"

"Oh, yes, if he can track him down. I'm worried sick."

Stacy was worried too. She worried the rest of the week. Neither Jane nor Alice heard from Gavin. He didn't call the shop, and he didn't call Stacy. A dozen yellow roses arrived on Friday with a card that said, *Put these in your room and imagine that I'm there too.*

Two tickets to the Braves/Padres game arrived on the following Monday, with a note that said, *I hope to be there, but if I'm not, take Mother. She'll love to watch you get excited. I do, too, but it's not the game that I'm thinking about.*

A Dracula and a Frankenstein video arrived Wednesday with a note that said, *Watch these and start with my neck. Then think of the rest of me and know that I'm very ready to be home with you.*

Each package was postmarked from a different place in the United States. Each gift made the waiting worse. Where was Gavin? What was he doing?

Jane and Alice ran an ad to sell the house.

The garage flourished.

The dogs languished.

The Braves won.

Stacy paced the floor and thought about boxer shorts with baseballs.

"Gavin, I'm a gambler, always have been. How else do you think a poor kid on the docks could acquire what I have?"

"I understand, Sol, but my little operation isn't big enough for you. You own shipping lines, casinos, resorts. Why on earth would you want an antique car restoration business?"

"Because of Lucky Lanham, boy, only because of him. He broke my daughter's heart. Now I'm going to do the same to his daughter."

"This is all because of Lucky Lanham?"

"It always was."

"But what if I come up with the money to pay you back?"

"You won't, and you won't find a banker willing to finance the rest of the deal either. It's me, or nobody."

"There's just one thing, Sol," Gavin played his last card. "I don't have the garage yet. She hasn't accepted my option money. So, even if you do take over the deal, you won't touch her."

There was a long, heavy silence before the olive-skinned man raised his eyes and concentrated their full force on Gavin. "So. You think that ends it? It only makes the gamble a bigger challenge. Tell you what, Magadan, I'll make you a deal."

"I don't think I'm interested in any more of your deals, Sol. I never should have taken your money to begin with. I did and I'll repay it, but I won't let you hurt Stacy."

"Oh, yes, you'll repay it all right, or I'll take

everything you own, including that mortgaged mansion your mother lives in on Valley Road. You know they ran an ad to sell it?"

Gavin cursed silently. He hadn't known. Jane hadn't known that the house was transferred to his name years ago, when he'd had to pay off the last mortgage to keep her from losing it. Now Sol was threatening to take the house, and he had the means to do it—the loan. Gavin owed Sol the money, and Gavin owned a house that could be claimed.

"So, what's the deal, Sol?"

"You get me that garage, and I'll forget about the rest of the land, and your house."

Gavin blanched. He couldn't take Stacy's garage. It was too important to her. Still, from the reports he'd received, it had become very successful in a short period of time. So what if the building went to Sol. They could find another building. He'd build another one in the center and give it to her. After all he was going to marry her, and what he had would be hers and what she had would be his.

"I'll do it, Sol. But I think you ought to know that I can't force Stacy to give up her business."

"Oh, I don't intend to deal with you, Magadan. You're welcome to be present, of course, but I'll only talk business with Lucky Lanham's girl. Go back to Hiram, Georgia, boy, and tell her that it's time she made good on her daddy's biggest debt."

Gavin felt like a jerk. He'd worked for years to be respectable, to make enough money to take care of his mother and his aunt, and then in a weak, self-indulgent moment he'd let his grand scheme to be a millionaire put him in a position to lose everything, including the woman he loved.

Sol never wanted to take over his business. Sol only wanted to get even with Lucky Lanham, and Gavin had given him the means to do it. Aunt Jane had always said there was some kind of force that tied people together, controlled their lives, and shaped their destinies. But Gavin had never believed it.

He still didn't.

He spent two hours feeling angry about what he'd done, then put his mind to a solution. Granted he had never made such a stupid mistake before, but he'd had worse situations to deal with in working through some of his mother's and Aunt Jane's wild schemes. He simply had to outsmart a crook, and he had three weeks to figure out how.

Now he had a baseball game to get to.

With one bite on the neck he'd become immortal. Night was coming, and he was in dire need of his life's blood—Anastasia Lanham.

Nine

Alice and Jane's spiritual center in downtown Atlanta was where Gavin caught up with Stacy. She was under the sink, repairing pipes that had gone unused for years.

For a long time he stood in the doorway, just looking at her. That was all it took for that satisfied feeling to steal over him, the promise that everything would be right, the warm spotlight of confidence.

"Whoever you are, I could use a hand down here."

"You can have it, Princess, and every other part of my body as well."

"Gavin!"

Stacy sprang up, banged her head against the open end of the pipe, and saw stars. "Ow!"

In an instant Gavin was beside her, hauling her out from under the cabinet, kissing the spot on her forehead that was already turning red.

"I'm so sorry. I really didn't mean to hurt you. Are you all right?"

Stacy looked into worried green eyes, stormy green eyes—Gavin's green eyes—and felt the connection reestablished. "I am now. Why did you leave me?"

"I had to. Business . . ." he offered lamely, his fingertips rimming her face as though he'd never seen it before.

"I know about that business, Gavin. I'm having a hard time keeping the home fires burning. We have to talk. We need to—"

"We need to get out of here before I do something that would embarrass my aunt and my mother."

"Not before we talk, Gatsby."

Gavin glanced around. The area just beyond the kitchen where Stacy had been working was crawling with workers. He shuddered to think what kind of wages his aunt had promised or what he'd have to do to stop this venture. He could hear Jane barking orders and his mother patiently explaining what it was that Jane wanted done.

The confusion fueled the emotional turmoil he'd gone through for the last week, and the confidence he'd felt seemed to vanish. Even Stacy couldn't make everything all right. He'd expected to find Stacy under the hood of a car or replacing brakes or mounting tires. Instead she was there, with his family, joining in their latest well-intentioned, but doomed-to-failure project. Stacy was becoming, not only a part of his heart, but his family as well.

Gavin smiled and nodded slowly. Stacy was right. He didn't want to talk about Sol and where he'd been. He wanted Stacy's comfort, her wonderful reassurance. He wanted her in his arms where they could make slow, beautiful love for hours. They could talk about horror movies and baseball, not trouble, not the collapsing of a dream. Like Lucky, he'd put on a brave face and shield her from the problem.

"Must we talk, Princess? I can think of better methods of making fuel."

Stacy recognized the look of pure frustration that claimed Gavin—recognized it and felt her heart lurch. She'd wanted him to face reality, to tell her what had happened, but she hadn't intended to cause him more pain. She'd been determined not to let him sidestep the issue by making love to her, but she missed the brash, take-on-the-world man she'd fallen in love with.

For a moment she caught her breath and held it. She was in love with Gavin Magadan. She wanted to hold him in her arms and make things right. She wanted to tell him to take the garage, it wasn't important. But she held herself in check, squelching her inclination to pull Gavin to the floor beside her and rip off his executive clothes.

She glanced down at her scruffy shorts and shirt and back at Gavin. This morning he was wearing a double-breasted business suit with a red paisley tie and a matching red handkerchief stuffed in his pocket. His shoes were dark brown with laces—imported, expensive, Italian. He looked like a man on a mission, but the expression on his face said plainly that it was a failed mission.

Well, it wasn't going to be like that. She had never committed herself to a man before, but without intending to she'd connected with Gavin Magadan. Just, she suspected, as Lucky had once connected with Jane. Lucky had run away. But she had no intention of letting some wild scheme, or misplaced male kind of protective thinking ruin what they had going.

From day one, fate had conspired to weave a spell that brought the two of them together. Stacy was willing to concede that there was something to be said for fate, but solutions depended on reasonable analysis and well-thought-out plans, and she intended to have a say in the outcome. Gavin Magadan belonged to her, and he wasn't about to close her out before she had a chance to make it work.

Gavin watched the myriad change of expression on Stacy's face. She wasn't going to let him protect her or change the subject. She wanted to talk, and no matter what he would prefer, they were going to talk. But not here, and not before he'd taken her in his arms. He couldn't hold back any longer.

He lifted her from the floor and kissed her, thoroughly, deeply, and with every ounce of longing he'd held back during all the hours they'd been apart.

And Stacy couldn't help herself. She kissed him back, giving as much as she got, entangling her arms around his neck and her fingers in his hair. She didn't give a thought to the grease she had on her hands, or the spot being transferred to his red tie. The sudden flurry of activity behind them didn't registered nor did the soft closing of the door.

Stacy gave up the pretense that talk was the first order of importance. When Gavin's hand slipped beneath her shirt and claimed her breast, little jabs of heat spiraled outward like a spring coiling tightly in her center.

The heating system wasn't working yet. They might never need it, Stacy thought crazily. All that was necessary was for Gavin to kiss her and the building occupants would have to open the windows in the coldest month of the year.

Then, insistently and steadily, Stacy was nudged back to reality. "Gavin," she finally whispered, "this isn't the dance floor."

"I know," he admitted, "and there aren't any bushes outside where I can ravish you. I guess we'll have to make do with what we've got. I'm willing to improvise."

"I think we'd better take what you've got home and ice it down," Stacy said, drawing away. "Lonnie always made me eat my peas before I could have dessert."

"Stacy, I'd like to call to your attention that I don't have any peas."

"In this case, Gatsby, consider the peas conversation, and we're not skipping the main course."

Stacy started for the door.

"Wait, darling, those guys out there will be able to read my condition like a newspaper. You're going to expose me to the world."

Stacy opened the door, glanced at the wide-eyed workers beyond, and said with a little salute, "Read it and weep, boys. Come on, big guy, we've got to skip the headlines and start with the fine print."

"A girl after my own heart," Aunt Jane said with a long, drawn-out sigh.

"Somehow, I don't think that's the part she's after," Alice commented with a satisfied smile, and watched them walk out the door.

Frankenstein and Dracula glared at Gavin, withholding their customary wags of approval as they stared at him from beside the front door.

"Come on, boys, I was out of town—on business."

Both dogs continued to stand, making no effort to come any closer.

"I think they're letting me know that they're unhappy with me," Gavin said dolefully.

"Possibly," Stacy agreed. "They have uncanny intuition about undercurrents."

"Hell," Gavin said, realizing what he'd said and preparing himself for an onslaught. None came. He knew then that he was in big trouble.

"All right, Stacy, let's talk."

"Fine. The couch? Or the study?"

"The study. You know what will happen if we sit on that couch. Even the hounds from Hades wouldn't be able to stop me from touching you."

"I'll make some coffee."

"Make it strong and black."

"Fine."

The coffee was awful, but that was as it should be. By the time she'd poured it into cups and set it on the table before them, Gavin had removed his coat and tie, and unbuttoned his shirt. He was sitting hunched over resting his chin on his threaded fingers.

"I knew Sol from the office. He'd invest in real estate now and then, buy and sell an occasional office building. He invited me to Vegas on a gambling trip as his guest. Then one day he called me and said that he had a little money to invest and he wondered if I knew anybody interested."

The dogs sat down and waited, more relaxed but still alert.

"I should have known better. But I was so certain that I could find a banker who'd back my project that I closed my eyes to the coincidence. I took his money to take options on the land and to set up my project. If I could get the land, the zoning, and the plans, then the mortgage money would come."

"Except it didn't." Stacy sat across the table from him, holding her cup in a death-crushing grip in an effort not to reach across and touch the man who was bearing his soul and admitting his failure.

"No, not yet. And, Stacy, there's more. I should have known that this wasn't a big enough deal for Sol. It didn't make sense when it was happening. This is peanuts for a man like him."

"But he had a reason, didn't he?"

"Yes." Gavin raised his eyes, and the naked pain swept across Stacy like a tidal wave of icy despair.

"I know, or at least I've figured out that from the beginning, the kicker was—me."

"How'd you know?"

"I knew about Sol's daughter and my father. I knew that she loved him and defied her father to be with him. But there's one thing I know that you don't. After my father died, she killed herself, in her own bed, the same bed that Lucky died in."

Gavin groaned and lowered his eyes. The final piece fell into place. Stacy *was* Sol's target. She had been all along. He'd simply sat back and waited until he had the chance to take everything she cared about. He'd take her garage. He'd ruin Gavin and his family, and he'd enjoy every minute of his revenge.

"Well, I won't let him get away with it, Stacy. I won't let him hurt you. All I have to do is repay his loan, and I'll find a way to do that if I have to sell everything I own."

He stood, gathered up his coat and tie, and

strode toward the door, ignoring the dogs who planted themselves firmly in front and bared their teeth in warning that he shouldn't try to get past.

"No, Gavin. Don't do this. I'm involved as much as you, more so. It's our problem. Two people who love each other work together. We can do it."

"Love each other?" He turned. "A man who loves a woman doesn't take, he gives. I'll be back when I've found an answer."

This time the dogs stepped aside and let him through. They let Stacy through as she dashed after him, catching him at the convertible, which was gleaming like hot coals in the sunlight.

"Gavin, wait. I need you to do something for me before you go. Please?"

He pitched his jacket onto the seat of the car and turned slowly around. "What?"

"Kiss me."

The kiss was desperate. It was wild and filled with longing. And at the end it trailed off into good-bye. Finally Gavin lifted his head and took a long, deep look into Stacy's eyes.

"Make me a bet, Stacy."

"A bet?"

"Sure, bet me two dollars that I'll be coming back."

"But I always win."

"I know. I'm counting on it."

But he didn't come back. Two weeks went by. The garage flourished. The Shelter for the Spiritual Odyssey of Man, and woman, too, began to come together. Donations suddenly started arriving. Volunteers turned up in every conceivable shape and form. There were writers who took on the shelter as their project for literacy. There were doctors who offered medical help. And the mayor appropriated funds for job retraining.

From their original plan to read tarot cards and offer spiritual guidance, Jane and Alice suddenly found themselves at the helm of a ship that was breaking new ground in the waters of the down-trodden.

The Braves won their division.

And Stacy paced her room at night and the garage by day.

"Lonnie," she finally said, "I'm desperate. What am I going to do?"

"If you're pregnant, I'll get my shotgun. Even Jane's nephew can't compromise my godchild and get away with it."

"That's not what I mean."

"Then what do you mean, Stacy? Let me hear your explanation as to why you're sitting here driving us all crazy, and Gavin is on his way to Vegas determined to take Sol on his own turf."

"Take Sol? How?"

"He's sold everything he owns. He's going to gamble for the money to pay Sol."

"Gavin? Gavin's no gambler, at least not that kind of gambler. He'll lose and not solve anything. Why would he even think of doing such a thing?"

"I think he's in love."

"Well, so am I, but I wouldn't—I couldn't—I mean, I'd lose. The Lanhams always lose when it's something important. Look at Lucky!"

"Yep, look at Lucky. And look at you. At least Lucky never turned his back on life. He always lived it to the fullest, and if he were standing right here, he'd tell you that he made mistakes, but he wouldn't change a thing."

"But what if I tried and ended up with nothing?"

"What do you have now, Anastasia Lanham? And better still, what if you won?"

For the rest of the day Stacy warred with the question. What did she have? Her garage was thriving. She had found new friends who were willing to share her good times and her bad. Her life had suddenly become meaningful, at least until Gavin had kissed her that last time and left. She'd never understood about belonging and commitment. She'd never known the physical well-being that came with the loving—not just satisfaction, but that warm glow that stayed with you through the day, that said the world is good, not perfect maybe, but manageable.

Gavin had never meant to cause pain. If he had, he'd have put restraints on his mother and his aunt years ago. Instead, he'd understood and supported them when he could, and rescued them when he couldn't. Acceptance and believing, that was what made Gavin special.

That and his boxer shorts with the baseball print.

And his lips and arms and—

Stacy went home and started making plans. Gavin had left for Vegas that morning. If she caught a plane that night, she ought to be there before complete disaster occurred. Vegas never closed, but serious gambling was still a late-night affair. And she was definitely into late-night activities.

Fortunately a few people still owed Lucky favors, and it was time for Stacy to call in one of them. She called a nearby airport and managed to hitch a ride on a friend's night courier flight to Vegas. Carefully Stacy packed her clothes, with-

drew the money she'd sworn she'd never touch—
the last of Lucky's gambling cache. Leashing the
dogs, she drove the truck to the small local airport
where private and small commercial aircraft were
based. The plane was waiting, and by eight o'clock
they were sliding through a moonlit sky on silent
wings.

The dogs cooperated, as did a tail wind, and
before nine o'clock Vegas time they were checking
into Sol's Lucky Dollar Casino. Used to everything, the clerks took Stacy's regal entrance as an
everyday event. The vicious-looking black rottweilers walked on either side of the elegant young
woman as if Vegas were old Petersburg and they
were auditioning for a remake of *Dr. Zhivago.*

Through the glittering lobby, past the huge
silver-dollar slot machine that gave the casino its
name, past awestruck patrons and glassy-eyed
players, Stacy walked slowly toward the eleva-
tors. Sooner or later Sol would learn that Lucky
Lanham's daughter was there, but there were so
many special hotel guests that she doubted the
desk clerk would alert Sol right away. Stacy
wanted to test the waters first, take a trial run.
Anastasia Lanham had come to gamble, and she
meant to break the bank.

Her knees were knocking. Her breathing was
coming fast and clumsy. Trying desperately to
hold down the unwelcome rise of excitement, she
moved slowly, her lips plastered in a smile that
was so tight, her teeth hurt.

Three more steps and into the elevator. She'd
made it, without seeing Gavin or Sol. She didn't
want to see Gavin yet either. She couldn't stop
him from what he was planning to do, and she
didn't want him to try to stop her. Running on the

raw edge of fear, she knew that it was going to take every ounce of control for her to get through the evening.

The bellman opened her door and led her inside, turning on the lights. It was not just any suite, but Lucky's regular suite. Of course she couldn't afford it, but by the time she left she'd either have the money, or Sol would own everything. One night in a hotel suite would be peanuts to a man like Sol. Stacy ordered the dogs to sit and reached for a tip. She needed something to keep her mind occupied as she surveyed the familiar surroundings.

There'd been a time when she'd thought she was in fairyland being there with her handsome father, following him around the gambling rooms and accompanying him to Sol's private quarters, the quarters where the big stakes games were held, by invitation only. Until she'd begun to understand what it meant to lose.

Lucky had never let her see the downside of his glamorous lifestyle until she'd come with him to Las Vegas. Then she'd known that gambling was an addiction, a promise, the allure of the dream. When a gambler lost, it was more than the loss of money, more than the loss of a dream, it was like dying a little more each time the disappointment came. And for Lucky, the disappointment had come more often, and the dying had been too painful to watch.

Until finally Stacy had gone home and had waited for the call that had come too soon. Lucky had died. But Stacy knew that Lucky had really lost a long time ago when baseball didn't need him anymore. Every bet he'd made after that had been his way of thumbing his nose at life which had taken both his loves—his wife and his physical ability to play the game he loved.

In the end, Stacy had been the only thing left he'd really cared about. For by then, Lucky had known it was too late.

A maid appeared at the door to unpack Stacy's clothes and gather those that needed pressing. On leaving, she reminded Stacy of the hotel's customary invitation to all suite occupants to be its guests for dinner.

Stacy called the desk and asked that someone come upstairs and walk Frankenstein and Dracula while she dressed. Moments later an ashen-faced employee took a leash in each hand and left with the boys accompanying him unwillingly.

Once alone, Stacy collapsed on the bed and took long, deep breaths. From beneath her blouse she fished her lucky coin and held it tightly. She didn't know who the patron saint of gambling was, if there was one, but she knew that she needed all the help she could get.

"Oh, Lucky, if you're up there anywhere, I could sure use a little edge."

There wasn't even a tinkle to indicate that he'd heard her.

Delaying the inevitable wasn't going to help. Stacy finally gathered her courage and marched into the bathroom. She discarded her traveling clothes, covered her dark brown hair with a shower cap, compliments of the hotel, and washed away as much tension as she could with a sharp spray of hot water.

Wrapped in a blanket towel, she blotted every drop of water from her skin, poured scented lotion into her palm, and applied it to the body she'd felt so inferior, until Gavin had touched it with his magic hands.

Gavin. She wondered where he was and what he was doing. Then, resolutely, she put him out of her mind and began to dress. She wore no bra. Her dress, with its strapless bra built in, would stand alone. Brief wisps of lace made up her panties. She wore self-supporting sheer red stockings that ended in a band of lace at her thigh.

Pulling on a short robe, she padded to the dressing table and started on her face. First she curled her hair with the curling iron. Big hair, the girls from Texas called it. High fashion the models in their designer gowns would have said.

A mess, Stacy thought, then continued with her make-over. She might never have passed her vamping certification, but it wasn't because she didn't have the equipment, or the experience in using it. She did. But she'd given up this kind of life six years earlier.

Stacy knew that you never gave a sucker an even break. She skillfully applied concealer, makeup, and eye shadow. Finally she clipped a great waterfall of red rhinestone earrings on her ears. What she looked like wouldn't have anything to do with her winning, but confusing or distracting her opponent wouldn't hurt.

And, she decided as she finished off her creation with lip gloss and blush, she was Lucky Lanham's daughter, and she intended to make him proud. Stepping into the red-jeweled gown, she slid the zipper into place and stepped back to view the results.

Yes. She might never be beautiful, but she was Anastasia, and Anastasia was majestic. Stacy intended to see that every man in the house knew it.

When the dogs were returned, she clasped matching rhinestone collars around their necks and replaced their leather leashes with velvet.

Taking one last look in the mirror, she fastened her lucky silver dollar around her neck and, tucking her jeweled purse beneath her arm, she left the room.

In the lobby every guest stopped and gaped at the woman exiting the elevator. Even Elizabeth Taylor couldn't have set a more glamorous stage. With a silent command to her bodyguards, Stacy walked through the gambling rooms to the restaurant, where she was shown to the best table in the house.

After a leisurely meal that she couldn't have identified afterward, Stacy left the restaurant and walked through the tables, studying the games without appearing to do so. Finally she settled at the roulette table. The odds were in favor of the house, but for her purposes, that was fine.

Stacy exchanged her money for dollar chips and started to play, only one bet at a time and for only a dollar. The stack of chips before her rose steadily. Stacy ignored the other gamblers, who urged her to increase her bets. Finally, she gathered up her earnings and cashed them in. In less than an hour she'd turned one dollar into three hundred.

The blackjack table proved equally generous. By midnight she'd won over five hundred dollars without losing one bet.

As she called to the dogs she was intercepted by a uniformed hotel employee who handed her a note. Unfolding the paper she glanced inside.

Sol knew she was here.

He was inviting her to join him at a private poker game in progress in his quarters.

Stacy took in a long, deep breath and nodded.

Moments later she was exiting the private key-operated elevator which led to the penthouse suite.

The music and noise of the downstairs gambling parlors was gone. Only the sound of rippling water and the low murmur of conversation broke the stillness. Stacy, Frankenstein on one side and Dracula on the other, followed the employee across the lush white carpet past an indoor waterfall and into the room where the game was being played. She paused in the doorway and surveyed the men around the table.

There was a gasp and everyone turned toward her.

She recognized two bankers from her time with Lucky, a famous game-show producer, and Sol, who raised his eyebrows in undisguised glee. In the shadows, wearing a grim look, was Gavin.

Ten

"Ah, Stacy." Gavin stood and held out his hand. "You're late, darling."

Darling? Stacy was nonplussed. She hadn't know what to expect, but a charming welcome came as a surprise.

As Gavin reached her side, the dogs cocked their heads anxiously, waiting for Stacy to signal their expected behavior. But it was Gavin who took their leashes from Stacy and directed the dogs to a spot near the door. "Sit! Stay!"

After a nod from Stacy, they complied, but gave every indication that they were ready to spring forward at any excuse.

Gavin struggled with a fierce need to jerk her up and carry her from the room. He used the dogs to buy time while he searched for a way to keep Sol from carrying out his threat to punish Stacy. He didn't know how Stacy had found out where he was and what he was doing, but knowing that she'd followed him made his heart swell.

"Thank you for coming to wish me luck, Stacy.

Would you like to have a drink before I escort you back to your room?"

Even now as she glared at him, he felt the warmth of her touch steal across his fingertips and spread up his arm. For a moment their gazes met and locked, then defiantly Stacy turned away.

"Hello, Sol," she said, "it's been a long time."

"Yes, it has, Ms. Lanham. I believe you know all the players?"

Stacy tried to put Gavin's lethal look of fury out of her mind as she nodded at each man and made her way around the table to Gavin's empty chair. "I'll take your chair, Gavin darling. I'm sure you won't mind sitting out the next hand."

"Would it matter if I did?"

"Yes, but it wouldn't stop me."

Eyes suddenly lit up as the men realized she intended to play. The other players slid back in their chairs and picked up their cards. Stacy took Gavin's hand and quickly calculated that he couldn't possibly win with the cards he was holding. When the bid came to her, she pitched the cards to the table. "Gavin's out."

The game-show producer took the hand, and the deal.

"I was afraid you might not come, Stacy," Sol went on, "but I see you're still your father's daughter."

"Not necessarily. When I play cards, I win."

"Aren't you afraid you're out of practice? I can't imagine that running a garage would keep the fingers nimble."

Gavin felt a flood of recriminations sweep over him. Sol had planned all of this, even the game. He'd given Gavin the chance to win his freedom, gambling that Stacy would come. He'd already won and they hadn't played a hand of poker. Gavin knew how Stacy felt about taking risks, and yet she was there, for him. What had he done?

"You'd be surprised what Stacy does with those fingers to keep them in shape," Gavin said, smoothly capturing Stacy's bare shoulder with his hand. "Did you get checked in all right, Princess?"

Just a touch and the connection was reestablished. Stacy let out a tight breath. Good, he wasn't going to refuse her help. "Oh, yes, *darling*. Now sit and quit fidgeting so I can concentrate."

Gavin studied his stack of chips and grimaced. He hadn't done badly, but he hadn't done well. The money he'd brought along wouldn't begin to support high stakes gambling for the two of them. Stacy wasn't going to give up without a fight, and if she were right about never betting more than ten dollars because she'd lose, this might be a short game. Still, he didn't want her to be embarrassed or do something foolish before he could talk to her. He slid his chips over to her position. "Go get him, Stace. You can do it."

"Thanks, Gavin, and I have a little money of my own." With that she opened her purse and took out a roll of bills.

Gavin hid his surprise. Where had she gotten so much cash? He watched her exchange it for chips and turn to face Sol with a challenge that even he couldn't miss. Sol's eyes stayed glued to Stacy's silver dollar that had turned sideways and was caught between her breasts.

Gavin had known she was beautiful beneath the coveralls. He'd known she was beautiful in faded shorts and a T-shirt. He'd seen her in a simple designer dress and flat shoes. But the woman he was watching now was sheer royalty and sultry sexuality.

"Deal, boys. What's the game?"

"Since you're the lady, you name it," the producer said graciously.

"Stud poker, five-card draw. Bet in ten-dollar increments only."

"Ten-dollar increments?" Sol looked around the table and back at Stacy as if he thought she had some trick up her sleeve. "I never heard of such a thing."

"I thought we were going to gamble," the banker complained.

"We will," Stacy promised, with only a slight tremor in her voice. "But I've been away from the table for six years. It won't hurt you guys to humor me for a while." She leaned forward, stretching the dress's limitations to the maximum. The silver dollar popped out of its resting place and hit the table with a clink. "Just until I get myself back in sync, men."

Gavin felt his stomach lurch and fought back the urge to jerk her out of that chair, throw her over his shoulder, and march out the door. One look at Sol told him that was exactly what their enemy was daring him to do. Gavin felt as if he were caught between a boulder and a steel wall.

She was game, Gavin thought, and courageous, coming here to do the one thing she'd sworn not to do—gamble. Still, she was hedging her bets. Limiting the bet to ten dollars might give her the confidence to win, but they'd be there from now until next year before they'd win enough money to pay Sol off.

Gavin glanced around at the other men. Wearing dinner jackets and diamond jewelry, they put their wealth on display. But what Stacy couldn't see were the men he was sure were standing just behind the doorway—big men with guns, mean enough to enforce whatever rules Sol chose to make. He groaned and tightened his grip on Stacy's shoulder.

He'd never felt so hopeless. There was no longer any doubt in his mind that he loved this woman, and he couldn't protect her. He'd gone blindly into a scheme that could cost her everything, cost him everything. Now she was there, ready to take a chance like none she'd ever taken, not for herself but for him.

His heart hurt, and he fervently wished that he could go back to that day in the garage and start everything all over.

Then Gavin felt her hand covering his, reassuring him. She was rubbing it gently, telling him with her touch that everything would be fine. But this time Gavin knew that their connection, their special sense of well-being, wasn't enough. For a moment he thought of Aunt Jane and wished for a little of her psychic ability. If not that, some of the fate that had conjured up such a match would be welcomed.

In the other room the sound of the waterfall tinkled happily. The dogs moved occasionally causing their collars to jingle. A waiter appeared from nowhere to add ice and refresh their drinks. When they reached Stacy's side, she shook her head in refusal. Other than touching Gavin's hand she remained absolutely still, absolutely regal.

"Very well," Sol agreed, passing the cards to the producer who shuffled them clumsily. "No limit to

the pot, but the bets must be in ten-dollar increments."

Stacy would have preferred a limit to the pot,
but she knew she'd pushed her advantage already. Now it was time to find out how lucky this
Lanham was. She gave a useless tug to her dress.
It didn't move. That was probably for the best. If it
wouldn't come up, it wouldn't go down. Every eye
at the table followed her movement, including
Gavin's whose accompanying pinch was duly
noted by Stacy as the producer began dealing the
cards.

Once around, hole card facedown. Pause.

The dealer turned up the next card for each
player. Stacy drew a four, Sol showed a nine, one
of the bankers a six of diamonds, the other a
queen, and the producer a jack. Oops, that made
Stacy's possibilities a bit more risky.

Everybody took a quick look.

Stacy had a jack of clubs. She reviewed her
memory. At this point the hole card meant nothing. In stud poker the player received five cards
with only the hole card hidden. It was too early yet
to speculate on possible combinations.

"High card bets," Sol announced, and watched
the banker holding the queen throw out a bill. The
others followed suit.

When play had returned to the dealer, there was
still less than two hundred dollars in the pot. The
third round of cards was dealt.

An eight of spades to the producer; a three of
clubs to the banker holding the queen, who
promptly threw in his hand; a seven of diamonds
to the second banker, possible straight; a second
four to Stacy, who let out a half breath; and a

second nine to Sol. Two pairs showed, but Sol's nine's were higher than Stacy's four.

"Pair of nines bets," Sol said. "I'll put in ten and raise you ten."

"I'll stay," the remaining banker said, "just for practice."

"I'll see your tens," Stacy said, "and I'll raise you two more tens."

Sol looked at the other players and lifted his eyebrows in astonishment. But Gavin realized what she was doing. She was only dealing in increments of ten dollars. He didn't know how long Sol would let this go on, but at least she wasn't likely to be wiped out instantly.

The producer folded.

The betting continued. Stacy was beginning to feel the tension. She'd been through this so often with Lucky, hovering in the background trying not to reveal her anxiety, watching her father cover his disappointment when he lost by making even more reckless bets on the next hand. But this was her first time to feel the pressure herself.

She felt Gavin's hand begin to move slowly, twisting until their fingers were intertwined. They were down to the last card. Sol now had three nines and a queen. Stacy had a jack in the hole, one showing, and two fours.

For a second she chewed on her lower lip as Sol bet. Then, feeling Gavin's touch, she nodded and added more tens to the pile.

In slow motion, Sol slid her final card across the table and turned it up. A jack. She'd drawn it, a full house. But there was still Sol to contend with, Sol and the Lanham curse. Would she win, or would she, like Lucky, lose a bet that, though low for the table, was of monumental importance to her?

Sol didn't show any emotion when the last card was dealt. A deuce. So Stacy still didn't know. Everything depended on his hole card. Everything depended on her luck.

Gavin marveled at Stacy's coolness. He thought for a moment that the Braves could use her on their ball team. The race for the pennant wouldn't rattle her. And she was probably as good at baseball as she was at poker.

Sol flung three tens into the pot and said, "All right, Stacy, we've let you have a practice round, now let's see what we've got."

"Fine." Stacy matched his bet. "Show me."

Stacy held her breath as Sol turned over his hole card. A king. No help. He only had three of a kind. Stacy let out a deep sigh of relief and looked up at Gavin with triumphant excitement in her eyes, as she said, "You turn it over, darling."

Gavin didn't have to. He knew what he'd find. A jack. A full house. Stacy had won the pot, and she'd done it on her terms.

"Thank you, Sol," she said as she gathered up the money. "For indulging me. This was only a test, a warm-up for the big match tomorrow night."

"Tomorrow night?" He frowned and leaned back in his chair. "Why wait?"

"Why not? I understand anticipation is half the fun of gambling, isn't it? Besides, I want you to have all day tomorrow to worry."

"But then, my dear, so will you."

"Now, suppose you tell me what you're doing here?"

Gavin was holding her arm in a painful grip, practically dragging her into the elevator.

"Not now, darling," she said with a purr in her voice. "I never give away my strategy in advance." Stacy blinked her eyes wildly and raised her gaze toward the corner of the elevator.

Belatedly Gavin followed her lead and noticed the almost hidden camera that was recording their movements.

"I just wasn't expecting you until tomorrow," he said smoothly, "but I'm glad to see you." He turned her into his arms with a motion that said he knew they were being watched. "Very glad."

Without making an obvious scene she couldn't avoid his kiss, she told herself as his lips claimed hers. Sol should believe they were so besotted with each other that they would be easy marks, she rationalized as her lips parted involuntarily, welcoming the invasion by the man whose tongue was giving new meaning to the term sneak attack.

The dogs relaxed.

Stacy and Gavin forgot about Sol, the camera, and their reason for being in Vegas. Wild hot kisses were given and received. Heated hands touched and stroked. The elevator opened and they were in the lobby. Neither had punched a floor button. As the sounds from the casino sifted through, Gavin finally lifted his head and looked around. Stacy's face was flushed. Her breathing fast. Her eyes like hot cider sprinkled with fire-light.

"Uh, Princess, I think we've arrived."

"Not yet, Gatsby, but five will get you ten that we will."

"Frankenstein! Dracula! Come!" Gavin took

Stacy's hand and led her across the lobby, the dogs trotting dutifully behind.

Two gamblers, who'd had a bit too much to drink, stared at Stacy and let out long, low whistles. "Elvira and her ghouls," one said. "Do you think they're real, or are we having an hallucination?"

"Hallucination," the second one said confidently. "Frankenstein is eight feet tall, and Dracula wears a cape. What we saw was a couple of midgets."

Gavin found a small spot of grass, encircled by flowers and hugging a fountain. The dogs investigated the flower beds, satisfied that Stacy was content to rest her head against Gavin's shoulder.

"Now," Gavin said, turning her to face him. "We talk."

"No talking, Gatsby, only wild loving. I'm tired of playing it safe and hiding from what I am."

He surveyed her gown from the slit in the skirt to the nothing piece of fabric that was trying to cover her nipples. "Anastasia Lanham, you're hiding very little tonight, very little."

"Actually," she said, laying her palms on the collar of his tux and staring up at him with a look that said he could proceed to go and collect anything he wanted. "Actually, I'm not hiding anything. You're looking at everything I'm wearing right now."

"Lordy, Stacy, you're vamping me into a state of no return."

"Good. Come boys! Heel!"

The dogs immediately fell behind as Stacy started back inside the hotel, and into the elevator, where she pressed the button for her floor.

"Try not to choke me," Gavin said.

"Choke you?"

"With that invisible leash you've slipped around my neck."

"Oh, is that what's holding us together? I thought it was some kind of energy field."

She handed Gavin her key and waited as he opened the door. Now that she'd let herself show him how she felt and what she wanted, she was having second thoughts. Suppose he didn't like Anastasia, the gambler. Suppose her new glamour was old hat to a playboy like Gavin? Suppose he didn't want to stay with her?

Gavin closed the door behind her and gave out a low whistle. "Wow, you sure know how to set the scene, Princess."

"I just wanted to pull it off."

"So did—do I—after we talk."

She turned to face him and lifted her eyes. "Do you really want to talk right now?"

The savage look of desire in her eyes zapped him, taking his breath away. "No, no, I think I can wait for talk, but not for you."

He found the zipper and slid it down with a soft swish. The dress fell to the floor in a glittering pool of red around her feet.

Her hair was a mass of dark-feathered curls, touched with lemony light. Her body took on a translucent golden color. The only things Anastasia Lanham was wearing beneath her gown were the thigh-high red stockings, lace panties, and the silver dollar on the chain around her neck.

Gavin knew she was breathing because he could see the rise and fall of the silver dollar. He wasn't certain about himself.

They claimed each other fast and furiously, reaching out in wild longing, their bodies saying what their minds were not yet able to express.

Later as she lay beneath him, breathless and filled with warmth, she allowed her eyes to meet his.

"I want you to know, Gavin, that no matter what else happens, *this* matters," she said. "What happens at the gambling table doesn't."

"That's your heart talking, Princess, not your mind."

"I'm learning to listen to my heart. I think perhaps it's wiser about some things. It took me a long time to understand that."

"You've been around Mother and Aunt Jane too long," Gavin said resolutely. "They've corrupted you."

"Nonsense, they've simply learned that life is to be lived, not regimented. Lucky understood that too."

They were sprawled across the still-made bed in Stacy's suite, limbs entwined, bodies fraught with the scent of lovemaking and the satisfaction of having been loved well.

"Now," Gavin said seriously, "what are you doing here?"

"The same thing you're doing here. "I'm just better equipped to do it."

"Gavin reached out and put his hand on her breast. "If you mean knocking the eyes out of those poor unsuspecting men, I'd say you have the right equipment."

"I meant gambling. I don't know how good I am, Gavin. I never gambled for money, only with Lucky. But he taught me well. When we played for matchsticks, I always won."

"From what I've heard about Lucky's gambling, that wouldn't have been hard to do."

"He didn't always lose. When he wasn't desperate, he could win. He was lucky. He just wasn't smart. Or, lately, I've been thinking that maybe he was smarter than I suspected. He was sick. Nobody knew but him. Something was beginning to affect his thinking and, in the end, he didn't care anymore."

"I can understand that," Gavin said softly. "I think I got desperate too. I'd always thought I would make my first million by the time I was thirty. When I hadn't, I guess I caught a case of Get Rich Quick. Now, I don't care anymore. Money isn't as important as it once was."

"I thought your classic car idea was pretty far-out," Stacy admitted, "but from the work orders and the telephone calls we are already getting, I've changed my mind."

"Oh, I never doubted the plan," Gavin admitted. "I just was in too big a hurry. I'm afraid it's a Magadan characteristic. I've always dealt with people who were movers and shakers, and it's easy to maneuver when you're using other people's money. I should have taken my time. I've learned my lesson about jumping into something before I'm prepared."

"Is that so?" Stacy shifted beneath his touch and stretched to reach his chin with her lips. "Then how do you account for our being on top of the sheets instead of underneath them."

"I think you know I was talking about business. This, my darling, is personal. Purely personal." He pulled her over him and claimed her nipple with his lips.

"Ahh! I don't think this would be considered a moment of purity by Lonnie. In fact, given the opportunity, I suspect that Lonnie wouldn't be above forcing a shotgun wedding if he thought you'd done me wrong."

Wedding? Gavin felt an incredible wave of new warmth sweep over him. That stupid smile had to be covering his face again. He and Stacy had been connected from the beginning, now they were committed, and that thought brought him nothing but pleasure.

"You're pregnant?"

"No, at least not so far as I know. But I have no intention of living in sin. Lucky might have run away from your aunt, but I'm a Lanham who goes after what she wants. Once we're done settling with Sol, I expect you to make an honest woman out of me."

"You mean when *I* get done settling with Sol. Right now, the only situation *we* have to deal with is looking for this solution." He lifted her even higher, then lowered her, joining them together in such a way that he felt as if their souls were touching.

Later, as she collapsed, sated and drained on top of him, she asked the question that had been nagging at her all evening. "Why did you greet me as if you'd expected me?"

"When I saw you in that doorway, looking like a cross between Cher and Madonna, I knew that I had to claim you or one of those men would try to ravish you right there on the table."

"Gavin, I'm a much more private person than that."

"Yes, but I'd have had to defend your honor. I'd probably have been challenged, the dogs would have attacked, and I might have suffered mortal injury in the melee."

"You forget, darling, I made you immortal. You're mine forever."

"Forever?"

"Forever."

But Gavin knew forever depended on his finding a way to get both of them out of the poker game. Long after he felt Stacy relax into sleep, he lay basking in the afterglow of their lovemaking. He didn't know what he was going to do, but he knew that he had to be the one to do it. He'd made the mess, not Stacy.

Stacy roused for a sleepy moment and planted one last satisfied kiss on Gavin's chest, as she whispered, "Ah, Gatsby, I love you so much. And I'm going to find a way to keep Sol from trying to destroy either of us."

That's what you think. Stacy was his heart. She was more important than Sol or his aunt's house or any amount of money. Even if Sol won that wouldn't end it. Sol wanted to punish Stacy, and the poker game afforded him an even better way to do that now. Once more, Gavin had given in to their enemy.

Gavin knew that only a fool would have missed the way he felt about Stacy. If there'd been any doubt, those kisses in the elevator and the fact that he was there, in her bed, would have been final proof. Sol had to know that he loved Stacy, and more—that she loved him in return. Now, by hurting one, he hurt the other. Everything was complicated. Everything except Stacy and Gavin's love for her.

Stacy was gone the next morning when Gavin woke. With distaste he climbed back into his wrinkled dinner clothes and made his way to his room, where he showered and sent his tux out to be pressed.

Yes, he was absolutely besotted with the woman. Yes, he agreed that she was perfect for his family and for him. Yes, he was sitting there hard and longing for her when he'd just spent most of the night making love to her.

After a pot of black coffee, he pushed those thoughts from his mind and began to study the possibilities. The only answer to the problem was money. With enough money he could repay Sol, pay off the mortgage on Jane's house, and protect the garage. The rest of the center could come later.

But, it took money to make money. And he didn't have nearly enough. Still, from little acorns came the mighty oak. He let out a deep sigh and dressed. He'd take what they had, and what they had was . . .

His pockets were empty. All his money was gone. Concentrating on Stacy's room, he could clearly see the empty dressing table where, at one point during the night, she'd emptied her purse and sprinkled the bills across the surface. Gavin had assumed when he left her room that Stacy was out walking the dogs. He'd been wrong.

Quickly he made his way to the lobby, scanning the gambling rooms, the slot-machine corridor, the restaurants. Nothing. Checking her room again, he found it empty. Stacy was gone.

"Disappeared early this morning," the desk clerk said, with a half-hidden smirk. "She charged her suite to you."

Gavin was stunned. His pockets were so empty that he couldn't even afford taxi fare to the airport to check the passenger lists. After giving a sob story to the travel agent in the lobby, he learned that no ticket had been sold to Anastasia Lanham. Gavin was confused.

By late afternoon he returned to his room, where he found a note from Stacy.

> Dearest Gatsby,
> When you read this you will know that I'm gone. You'll also know that I've taken your money. I wasn't certain that my luck would hold, but it did. Through the day I've covered the strip, turning our money into a stake worthy of a real challenge to Sol. I don't know if the Lanham luck has changed, or if it's just being connected to you that's made me lucky, but I feel right about this. Wait for midnight and sleep with the windows open.
> Stacy

Midnight? Sleep with the windows open? What was the woman talking about? What was she doing? Where was she?

Gavin couldn't answer any of those questions except what she was doing. That he understood. She planned to play cards with Sol again, high stakes, winner take all. He had to stop her. He had to tell her that he loved her, that he was willing to lose everything to protect that love.

Were they playing there, or somewhere else? Sol. Sol would know. But the switchboard said Sol was away for the day. And nobody would tell Gavin where, or if, a high stakes game was set for that night.

For the first time in his life Gavin was stymied. He'd reached a brick wall and couldn't even find a crack to let him get to the woman he loved. By evening he'd exhausted every possible lead. He finally resorted to charming the chambermaid into unlocking Sol's empty quarters so that he could confirm the plans for the evening. The table was being made ready. The bar was being stocked. The game was on—for eleven o'clock.

But how was he to get in? Gavin pondered the problem as he went back to his room. He would bet his last dollar, if he had one, that Sol would have a dozen look-alikes guarding the elevator and the penthouse. He'd have to find a way. Maybe from the roof. Maybe—

There was a knock on his door. Stacy might not plan to include him in the playoffs, but Sol had no intention of losing any of his advantage. An invitation to the game was being hand delivered by the same bellman who delivered Gavin's freshly pressed tux.

Three hours until game time, Gavin realized. He badly needed rest. There was nothing more he could do until eleven o'clock. He took off his clothes, determined to take a nap. But sleep was elusive. He wandered to the window and recalled Stacy's cryptic words to sleep with the windows open.

Of course. She intended to return to him at midnight. The reference was to their forever connection, the bite she'd given him on the neck, immortality. Gavin smiled. Aunt Jane was right. They were connected by a force that endured. He went back to bed and closed his eyes.

Across the street Stacy stared from her bedroom window, wishing she really did have wings that could carry her to Gavin's open window. Just knowing that he understood her reference gave her great joy. His open window was like Lonnie and Grace leaving the porch light on for her, a steady reassurance that he'd always be there, her anchor, her soul mate.

Stacy was very tired. She'd spent most of the night making love to Gavin and the entire day at the gambling tables, betting in ten-dollar increments, steadily increasing her funds until at last she had better than ten thousand dollars. The incredible run of luck was almost frightening. Lucky had longed for such power. She'd never cared about money.

She wasn't even sure she cared now, except for Gavin. If she could win enough to pay off Sol, they could share a life together without having the cloud of debt hanging over them.

She rippled the bills, thinking about what a monumental thing this small debt had become. Corporations dealt in billions of dollars without a thought. Countries were trillions of dollars in debt. In the scheme of things, winning a mere hundred thousand dollars didn't seem like much, but for her it was a measure of her future.

This time she didn't worry about distracting her opponents. Instead of wearing a dress that barely covered her body, she chose a long-sleeve green satin gown that covered every inch of her front, but plunged to a scandalous depth in back. Again she teased her hair into a dark brown cloud and sprinkled it with stardust held on with hair spray. She wore no jewelry, except for her lucky silver dollar.

Knowing the importance of making an entrance, she slid her small feet into four-inch matching green satin pumps that extended her height to almost six feet. Tonight the dogs were snapped into matching green satin collars and silver leashes. She sprayed on her favorite perfume and studied herself in the mirror. She looked mysterious and successful and lush.

Moments later she was entering the elevator to the penthouse. Just late enough for everyone to be there. Her money was carefully counted and ready inside the clutch purse beneath her arm. She gave the camera an open look and what she hoped was her most confident smile.

The door slid open to the sound of the waterfall. But there was no murmur of conversation, no tinkle of ice in glasses. The atmosphere was serious. She calculated that in no more than an hour she'd be able to return to Gavin, either triumphant or flat broke.

Into the room she strode, the dogs marching smartly beside her.

"Good evening, gentlemen!" Her eyes swept the waiting players—Sol, a stranger she didn't recognize, the same banker from the night before and—"Gavin!"

"Good evening, darling," he said smoothly, coming to her side with a ready kiss for her cheek. "You didn't think Sol would let me miss this, did you?"

Stacy swung around to Sol, a look of fury on her face. "This wasn't part of our agreement, Sol. Gavin wasn't supposed to be here."

"So, I lied," he said. "You can't blame me. All's fair in love and war—and revenge."

"Fine, you want to make this a war. Bring on the guns. Boys, sit!"

The dogs found their places by the door and crouched down.

Stacy took her seat at the table and waited for

Gavin's hand to clasp her shoulder. It did. She felt a surge of strength sweep through her and smiled. Opening her purse she took out her money and laid it on the table. Sol only nodded. That she was prepared didn't come as a surprise to him. She decided that he probably knew what she'd done all day, even though she'd been careful to avoid Sol's casino.

"Tonight you may choose the game," Sol said to Stacy, "but there will be no limit on the bets, nor on the pot. We play with thousand-dollar chips."

Stacy gulped. Up to now she'd played it safe by sticking within her ten-dollar limit. Now came the test. Could she do what she had to do? Gavin leaned down and under the guise of giving her a kiss, said, "Go for it, darling. If we lose, we'll go back to Hiram and I'll get a job in a hardware store to support my wife."

Wife? Stacy blanched, then pulled her attention away from that thought. First they had to get through this game, then she'd allow herself to think about Gavin's words. "Whatever you say, Sol. You're playing with Lucky Lanham's daughter, and she's come to break the bank."

The game was five-card stud, nothing wild. And by the end of the first hour she'd tripled her winnings. With each hand her confidence grew. The deal had worked itself back around to Sol, who announced a change in the game.

"Seven-card stud, deuces wild."

This time Stacy did gasp. Seven-card stud she could handle. Having three hole cards with deuces being wild was more of a challenge. But betting with thousand-dollar chips only gave her thirty chips to play with.

"That's why you came, isn't it?" Sol asked. "To challenge me?"

"No," Gavin interceded. While he'd made up his mind that losing wouldn't be a disaster, Stacy hadn't. She was taking a chance for him, but if she failed, she might be crushed by that failure. "Forget it, Stacy," he said sharply, "take what you have and let's go."

Stacy considered doing just that. She'd already made up her mind that the garage didn't matter. But in some weird kind of way the game had become a symbol. She was playing for Lucky, too, and if she quit now, she'd never know whether or not she could have won. And Gavin would lose everything, possibly even the Shelter for the Spiritual Odyssey of Man, and woman too.

"No, we've come this far, Gatsby, we're going all the way—together. Okay?" She looked up at Gavin, and he saw all the love he'd ever wanted shining in her eyes. The rest was in the hands of whatever fate had brought them this far.

"Okay, Princess."

Stacy's first hole card was a two of clubs. The second, dealt facedown was a four of hearts. She could hear Lucky giving her lessons. *Deuces are wild, Stace.* A deuce could also be the beginning of a straight, or a pair.

Her first show card was a five of hearts. She already had the four and a wild card. What were the odds that she'd draw either the two, three, or six of hearts? Probably slim, but a straight flush was the second highest hand any poker player could have.

The banker bet on his jack of spades. The stranger with the four of clubs stayed in.

Sol had drawn the two of hearts. Not only a wild

card, but the two of hearts she needed for her straight. That hurt. Now she'd have to draw the three and the six or another wild card.

After the next round, Stacy had a nine of diamonds, no help. The banker folded. Sol drew the queen of hearts.

"Well, now, this gets interesting," Sol said, "first the deuce, now the queen. Looks like I'm drawing your hearts." Then he turned up a six of hearts for Stacy. "What do you think, Magadan, could she have the three and four hidden? I think not. She's her father's daughter, and the Lanhams are losers."

"I warn you, Sol," Gavin said carefully, "Stacy is a strong woman who goes after what she wants. Don't confuse her with her father. Stacy doesn't lose."

"We'll see." Sol dealt himself the ten of hearts. "Queen still bets. Five thousand says I don't believe you can do it. What's it worth to you, Ms. Lanham?"

Stacy did some quick calculations. Her money was dwindling fast. What was she doing? Ever since Lucky had died she'd avoided anything that reminded her of the addiction that sucked every shred of respect from his life. Now, in a heartbeat, she'd suddenly became her father, risking everything.

Gavin felt the tension that turned her body into a statue carved from ice. He slipped his fingertips around her neck and tilted her head so that she could see him. For a long minute he simply looked at her. "Let's get out of here, Princess. Forget the money. I have to look for a job."

Stacy stared at him in surprise. Was he seriously suggesting that she walk away—that they throw in the towel? She couldn't, it mattered too much. She'd learned about how hard he'd worked to be somebody, and she wouldn't be responsible for his going back to that kind of life again. Fear gave way to pure determination. Of course Gavin couldn't work in a hardware store. She wouldn't lose.

Stacy's sixth card was the three of hearts. There was nobody in the game but she and Sol.

The room went silent. Stacy could only hear the sound of the dogs' collars clanking now and then and the waterfall in the other room, and her breathing.

"Well, now, Stacy. You have a three, a five, and a six of hearts showing. I have a queen, a ten, and a wild card. We appear to be gambling with hearts, just like my daughter did. Appropriate, don't you think?"

Stacy didn't dare breathe. Only the firm pressure of Gavin's hand on her shoulder gave her the strength to keep her expression bland. With her wild card she had her straight flush; two, three, four, five, and six of hearts. She had him, the wily old bastard. Unless he had a king and ace in the hole—or drew one. She waited.

"Deal your card, Sol. Stacy and I have a date," Gavin said lightly, and watched as Sol turned over the ace of hearts.

Stacy felt her heart plunge to somewhere in the vicinity of her toes. All Sol needed was the king of hearts, and he had two hole cards already, with one to go. She waited quietly.

"I think this is the end of the line, Stacy Lanham. I believe the time has come to see what you have. I think I'll bet the bank."

Stacy watched him shove his entire stack of

money forward. More than Stacy could begin to match. She could no longer feel her heart beating. The haze of smoke in the room gave a surreal air to the participants. For a moment she felt faint. How on earth could her father have survived this kind of life?

The answer was, he hadn't. And after this night, neither would she. Then she felt an infusion of strength as Gavin's other hand clasped her shoulder. Standing behind her, he was silently giving her his confidence, his boldness and daring. And then she understood. Alone, she was just a gambler with everything to lose. But Gavin loved her, and that love was a power to be reckoned with.

"Let's cut the crap, Sol," Gavin said in a low voice. "You set this up to ruin me and hurt Stacy. You've done it."

"No!" Stacy interrupted. "You know I can't match your bet, so I'll make you a new wager. What you have on that table against every penny I brought with me, Gavin's loan, and—my garage."

Sol looked at the cards and back at the woman he'd sworn to punish. "It's a bet!"

"No point in prolonging the agony, Sol. Let's see what we've got. He dealt her last card and turned it up (the six of clubs). Stacy's expression didn't waver.

Sol turned up his last card. The king of hearts. Smiling, he revealed his hole cards—a six of spades, and . . . the ace of hearts.

Stacy stared at the card in disbelief. He'd won. A royal flush, ace, king, queen, the deuce as a wild card for the jack, and the ten of hearts took her straight flush.

She'd lost. Just as Lucky had. The first time in

her life she'd gambled for something that really mattered, and she'd lost. Stacy came to her feet, took her purse, and turned away from the table.

"Just a minute," Sol said. "I think you've forgotten something."

"Forgotten something?" Gavin, using every ounce of self-control he possessed, spoke between clinched teeth. "If you're worried about the garage, you'll get the deed as soon as we get back to Georgia."

"No," Sol shot back, "Stacy said every penny she brought with her. I'll take the silver dollar around her neck."

Gavin felt a sudden rage sweep over him. "Now wait a minute, Sol, that silver dollar is a piece of jewelry. Her father gave it to her. You can't take that. It doesn't mean anything to you."

"*Hell* if it doesn't."

The dogs growled and started their charge.

"No," Gavin started to say, then stopped.

Before Sol knew what was happening both dogs had hit him from the rear, knocking him to the floor. The two other men quickly stepped back and watched Sol desperately trying to protect himself as Frankenstein and Dracula took the command, carrying it out beautifully.

The guards charged into the room and stared in disbelief.

"Shall we stop them, Stacy?" Gavin asked as the two dogs, their feet planted firmly on Sol's chest, began to lick.

"Not just yet," Stacy said as the absurdity of the situation began to sift through her shock. "I think Sol's soul needs a little cleansing, don't you?"

But the expression on Sol's face was one of

terror. "Get them off, Stacy. You can keep your garage, just don't let them kill me!"

"No, Sol," Gavin said, you won the bet fair and square. But we will keep the silver dollar. That's about what your life is worth. Frankenstein! Dracula! Sit!"

The dogs came to a reluctant stop and took their places on either side of Gavin and Stacy.

"Well done, boys. Shall we go, Princess?" Gavin gave a little bow.

Stacy curtsied and took his arm. "I believe I'm ready, Gatsby." Together they made a very royal exit from the room. Inside the elevator, Gavin collapsed into laughter.

"Did you see Sol's face when those dogs attacked him?"

Stacy, at first shocked by Gavin's behavior, began to see the humor in the situation and started to laugh too. By the time they reached the lobby, they were in each other's arms, kissing and laughing.

"You know we're completely broke, Gatsby."

"Completely, Princess." He kissed her in the middle of the foyer.

"How do we pay our hotel bills?"

"We don't. Let Sol eat them. How do we get home?"

She kissed him in the center of the corridor lined with slot machines. "The hotel van will take us to the airport free of charge, and we hitch a ride on a plane that belongs to a friend of mine."

"Then I think we've got it made, darling. I'm ready for some dirty dancing. How about you?" He started dancing her down the corridor between the slot machines, singing something about being broke and side by side.

"You know what happened the last time we danced," Stacy observed.

"Yep, and you know it's happening again. Want to find a bush and get naked?"

"Absolutely." She leaned her head back and let him whirl her past the startled gamblers and into the lobby.

"Whoa, Gavin," she said, coming to a stop in front of the huge slot machines that gave Sol's Lucky Dollar Casino its name. "We still have one coin left, my lucky coin. If we're going to start from scratch, we might as well be completely broke. She dropped it in the machine and turned back to face Gavin. "Now, pull the lever, and let's go find a preacher."

"Do you suppose we can find one who'll take a charge card?"

"So I changed my mind, we'll live in sin. I love you, Gavin Magadan."

"I love you, too, Anastasia Lanham. What do you want to bet that Lonnie will be waiting at the airport with a shotgun?"

"Bet? Me? Never again, I've learned my lesson." He loved her. She didn't need anything else.

"Oh?" He lowered his face, his green eyes flecked with stars from the myriad lights overhead. "And what lesson is that?"

She smiled and parted her lips to receive his kiss. "Take a chance on a lean, mean, loving machine."

Their lips touched in a searing flash of heat. Their bodies joined in an almost audible sigh of fulfillment, as Gavin pulled the lever.

His kiss was hard and demanding, and she accepted it, just as she'd accepted the man. Loving him was a gamble, the biggest gamble she'd ever made. She returned the kiss and asked for more, pledging her love with her embrace.

Behind them the giant Lucky Dollar slot machine whirled. In a haze of awareness Gavin saw strangers walking through the corridor stop to watch in amazement. He could understand that. Stacy was something to see.

Then he lost himself in her taste and touch. Bells began to ring. Sirens went off. The crowd began to ooh and aah. The dogs whined and pressed closer.

"Hey man, look at the zeros!"

"You've done it, dudes. For a year that machine has gobbled up every dollar it was fed and never even let out a burp!"

Gradually, the sounds sifted through his awareness. Gavin lifted his head and surveyed the astonished crowd who'd gathered and were staring at them.

"Princess. Princess, I think you'd better see this." He released Stacy and turned her toward the machine.

Dimly Stacy swam back to the present and tried to focus on whatever was more important to Gavin that kissing her. Then she saw it, the numbers on the machine. She couldn't even count that high.

"Did we win something?" she asked, impatient to recapture Gavin's attention.

"Did you win?" a casino employee said in astonishment. "If I read those figures right, you won the biggest payoff in the history of Las Vegas. Can you believe it?"

"Of course," she said with a knowing smile. "I knew that in the elevator. The money is just a little something extra, a wedding present from a man who knew that one day I'd need it."

"Little something? Stacy, darling, we're rich."

"We certainly are." Stacy glanced at her watch. "I think you'd better get us to the airport. It's close enough to the bewitching hour, my mate, and tonight there's a full moon."

Epilogue

"Jane has become an absolute scandal," Alice Magadan was saying to Stacy as she adjusted her bridal veil.

"Oh, how's that?"

"She and Lonnie. They're practically living together."

"I know," Stacy said dreamily, arranging her wedding gown. "I guess that Jane will wear this dress after all."

"I suppose. It's that other one I don't know what to do about." There was a little catch in Alice's voice, a tinge of worry that Stacy noticed at once.

"What other one, Alice? Nick?"

"Not Nick, he seems to be the only man who's not operating on his hormones. I'm talking about Jim. He thinks he's twenty-one and that I'm . . . available."

Jim, the farmer with the barns full of car parts, the fifth partner in Magadan Classics? Stacy thought. She'd been so in love that she hadn't even noticed their attraction. Yet in retrospect, it was inevitable. The aura of love that surrounded her and Gavin had spilled over everyone. Lonnie and Jane weren't dancing through the corridors and dashing into the bushes, but they weren't making any secret of their passion. Now Alice and Jim had caught the love fever.

"Well, aren't you?" Stacy said quietly to the blushing woman who would be her mother-in-law in less than an hour. "Available, I mean?"

"Stacy, I'm a senior citizen. But the old fool just keeps kissing me."

"I think that's wonderful, Alice. Gavin will be so pleased to know that you will experience even a little of what we have. Besides, your grandchild will need a steadying influence in this family. And Jim is about the only levelheaded one among us."

"Grandchild?" Alice turned to face Stacy, her expression beaming with joy.

"Yes, but don't tell Gatsby yet. It's my wedding gift to him, and he can't open my present until after the ceremony."

Alice giggled. "Stacy darling, I think you're a little late with that thought."

The wedding was held by the lake, at twilight, on a Saturday in October. The guests never understood the reason for the abbreviated ceremony, but Gavin did. They'd live together the rest of their lives, but the Braves might never again play in the World Series.

The punch was poured and the cake was quickly cut and served. Gavin hustled their guests out, stationed the boys beside the door, and started up the steps to the loft. He dropped his jacket on the banister, his shirt and bow tie fell on

Stacy's wedding dress on the first step, his trousers landed on her white silk stockings midway up, and his underwear joined hers at the top of the staircase.

His bride—no, his wife—was already waiting in the bed, gloriously nude, sprawled across the pillows like a princess ready to be adored. She'd brought a pitcher of punch, servings of wedding cake, peanuts, popcorn, and the TV.

"Five will get you ten that you're gonna overdose on dessert this afternoon, Gatsby."

"No more betting, Princess. This wager is a sure thing."

He fell across her, entering her, feeling the explosion of heat accelerate to the danger level. "Five will get you ten that your days of grease under the fingernails are numbered."

"Oh? Why is that?"

"Because I intend to keep you all to myself, barefoot and pregnant."

"Oh, that," she said airily, wrapping her legs around his. "You're really a little slow sometimes, my darling. Haven't you noticed? I gave up crawling under trucks a month ago." She lifted herself against him, filling his body with her passion and his mind with her words.

Like the slot machine in Vegas, bells clanged, oceans roared, fireworks detonated, the world whirled past, catapulting them into some hazy place that cushioned them in the soft afterglow of their loving.

It seemed like hours later that Gavin heard the playing of "The Star-Spangled Banner."

"Appropriate," he murmured. It wasn't even twilight, and he'd seen the rocket's red glare and heard a few bursting bombs too. But that was nothing new. He struggled to focus on something important, something . . . "You did? Stacy, you're pregnant? How?"

He rolled off her, catching her cheek with his fingertips and searching her face in alarm.

"I'm very pregnant, Gavin Magadan. The doctor said it probably happened that first night. Are you sorry?"

"Sorry? I've hit the jackpot. I'm the luckiest man in the world," he said, reverently laying his hand on her stomach. "A child of royalty, a lucky child. I'll bet it's a girl."

"That's one bet you'll lose, Gavin," Stacy said, snuggling into his arms. "Jane's tarot cards have already predicted that it's a boy."

"You don't really believe she can read those things, do you?"

"Nobody believed the Braves would make the World Series, did they? You just never know who fate will smile on."

But Stacy knew. She turned her face for a kiss. And she knew that someday there'd be another lucky woman who'd gamble on being loved by a lean mean loving machine.

THE EDITOR'S CORNER

What could be more romantic than weddings? Picture the bride in an exquisite gown. Imagine the handsome groom in a finely tailored tuxedo. Hear them promise "to have and to hold" each other forever. This is the perfect ending to courtship, the joyous ritual we cherish in our hearts. And next month, in honor of June brides, we present six fabulous LOVESWEPTs with beautiful brides and handsome grooms on the covers.

Leading the line-up is **HER VERY OWN BUTLER**, LOVESWEPT #552, another sure-to-please romance from Helen Mittermeyer. Single mom Drew Laughlin wanted a butler to help run her household, but she never expected a muscled, bronzed Hercules to apply. Rex Dakeland promised an old friend to check up on Drew and her children, but keeping his secret soon feels too much like spying. Once unexpected love ensnares them both, could he win her trust and be her one and only? A real treat, from one of romance's best-loved authors.

Gail Douglas pulls out all the stops in **ALL THE WAY**, LOVESWEPT #553. Jake Mallory and Brittany Thomas shared one fabulous night together, but he couldn't convince her it was enough to build their future on. Now, six months later, Jake is back from his restless wandering and sets out to prove to Brittany that he's right. It'll take fiery kisses and spellbinding charm to make her believe that the reckless nomad is finally ready to put down roots. Gail will win you over with this charming love story.

WHERE THERE'S A WILL . . . by Victoria Leigh, LOVESWEPT #554, is a sheer delight. Maggie Cooper plays a ditzy seductress on the ski slopes, only to prove to herself that she's sexy enough to kindle a man's desire. And boy, does she kindle Will Jackson's desire! He usually likes to do the hunting, but letting Maggie work her wiles on him is tantalizing fun. And after he's freed her from her doubts, he'll teach her to dare to love. There's a lot of wonderful verve and dash in this romance from talented Victoria.

Laura Taylor presents a very moving, very emotional love story in **DESERT ROSE,** LOVESWEPT #555. Emma Hamilton and David Winslow are strangers caught in a desperate situation, wrongfully imprisoned in a foreign country. Locked in adjacent cells, they whisper comfort to each other and reach through iron bars to touch hands. Love blossoms between them in that dark prison, a love strong enough to survive until fate finally brings them freedom. You'll cry and cheer for these memorable lovers. Bravo, Laura!

There's no better way to describe Deacon Brody than **RASCAL,** Charlotte Hughes's new LOVESWEPT, #556. He was once a country-music sensation, and he's never forgotten how hard he struggled to make it—or the woman who broke his heart. Losing Cody Sherwood sends him to Nashville determined to make her sorry she let him go, but when he sees her again, he realizes he's never stopped wanting her or the passion that burned so sweetly between them. Charlotte delivers this story with force and fire.

Please give a rousing welcome to Bonnie Pega and her first novel, **ONLY YOU,** LOVESWEPT #557. To efficiency expert Max Shore, organizing Caitlin Love's messy office is a snap compared to uncovering the sensual woman beneath her professional facade. A past pain has etched caution deep in her heart, and only Max can show her how to love again. This enchanting novel will show you why we're excited to have Bonnie writing for LOVESWEPT. Enjoy one of our New Faces of '92!

On sale this month from FANFARE are three marvelous novels. The historical romance **HEATHER AND VELVET** showcases the exciting talent of a rising star—Teresa Medeiros. Her marvelous touch for creating memorable characters and her exquisite feel for portraying passion and emotion shine in this grand adventure of love between a bookish orphan and a notorious highwayman known as the Dreadful Scot Bandit. Ranging from the storm-swept English countryside to the wild moors of Scotland, **HEATHER AND VELVET** has garnered the following praise from *New York Times* bestselling author Amanda Quick: "A terrific tale full of larger-than-life characters and thrilling romance." Teresa Medeiros—a name to watch for.

Lush, dramatic, and poignant, **LADY HELLFIRE** by Suzanne Robinson is an immensely thrilling historical romance. Its hero, Alexis de Granville, Marquess of Richfield, is a cold-blooded rogue whose tragic—and possibly violent—past has hardened his heart to love . . . until he melts at the fiery touch of Kate Grey's sensual embrace.

Anna Eberhardt, who writes short romances under the pseudonym Tiffany White, has been nominated for *Romantic Times*'s Career Achievement award for Most Sensual Romance in a series. In **WHISPERED HEAT,** she delivers a compelling contemporary novel of love lost, then regained. When Slader Reems is freed after five years of being wrongly imprisoned, he sets out to reclaim everything that was taken from him—including Lissa Jamison.

Also on sale this month, in the Doubleday hardcover edition, is **HIGHLAND FLAME** by Stephanie Bartlett, the stand-alone "sequel" to **HIGHLAND REBEL**. Catriona Galbaith, now a widow, is thrust into a new struggle—and the arms of a new love.

Happy reading!

With best wishes,

Nita Taublib
Associate Publisher
LOVESWEPT and FANFARE

In the Bestselling Tradition of Julie Garwood

HEATHER AND VELVET
by Teresa Medeiros

*A courageous beauty and her sensuous outlaw ignite fires of
passion that blaze from the storm-swept countryside to the wild
moors of Scotland . . . forging unbreakable bonds of love.*

One moment lovely Prudence Walker was living the
life of a dutiful orphan, the next she was lying in a
highwayman's arms. Wounded in a foiled robbery attempt, and thoroughly drenched from a storm, the
dreaded Scot bandit seemed harmless enough. Or so Prudence thought—until the infamous rogue stole her breath
and her will with his honeyed kisses, until she felt the
rapier-sharp edge of his sensuous charm.

She was everything Sebastian Kerr had ever wanted,
but could never have; an impish beauty with amethyst
eyes and wine-sweet lips he longed to plunder. But even as
he drew Prudence into his embrace, he knew he must
leave her. For the gray-eyed highwayman was leading a
dangerous double life, one that left no room for love. . . .

Prudence's mouth went as dry as cotton as the lantern flame shed a
halo of light over the highwayman's face. His tawny hair was badly
in need of a trim. She reached to brush it back from his brow before
she realized what she was doing. Snatching her hand back, she
inadvertently touched the hot tin of the lantern. She stifled a gasp
of pain, telling herself one burn was better than another.

Lifting the lantern higher, she hungrily studied his features. The
sun had burnished his skin to a warm, sandy color that nearly
matched his hair. His low-set brows were a shade darker. A thick
fringe of charcoal lashes rested on his cheeks. Aunt Tricia would do
murder for such lashes, Prudence thought. Not even copious

amounts of lamp black could duplicate them. His nose was slightly crooked, as if it had been broken once, but its menace was softened by the faintest smattering of freckles across its bridge. A pale crescent of a scar marred the underside of his chin. Shallow lines bracketed his mouth and creased his forehead. Prudence suspected they had been cut not by time, but by wind and weather. She judged his age to be near thirty.

The lamplight played over his mouth like a lover, and Prudence felt her chest tighten. It was a wonderful mouth, firm and well formed, the bottom lip fuller than the top. Even in sleep, the slant of his jaw tightened it to a sulky pout that would have challenged any woman. Prudence wanted to touch it, to make it curve in laughter or soften in tenderness.

She leaned forward as if hypnotized.

"Amethyst."

The word came from nowhere. Her gaze leaped guiltily from the bandit's lips to his wide-open eyes.

* * *

Prudence was caught in a trap of her own making, paralyzed not by the accusing circle of light, but by the stranger's eyes, which were the misty gray color of summer rain. She felt like a dowdy moth beating its wings against a star.

"Amethyst?" she repeated weakly. Perhaps the bandit was dreaming of gems he had stolen.

"Your eyes," he said. "They're amethyst."

She blinked. Prudence had no difficulty seeing things close to her, so there was no need to squint now. If she closed her eyes, she suspected she would still see his face, etched indelibly on the slate of her mind. He did not touch her, but she could not move. Poised there in the light, she waited for him to reproach her or yell at her or shoot her. She bit her bottom lip, then loosed it quickly, remembering how her aunt said the childish habit emphasized her buckteeth.

Sebastian studied her frankly, his earlier suspicions confirmed. The girl was utterly lovely. The delicate alabaster of her skin gave her even features a surprising fragility. A nearly imperceptible cleft crowned the tip of her slender nose, and the primness of that nose was belied by a faint overbite that hinted at an alluring pout. Stubby dark lashes framed her violet eyes. The lamplight sought out burgundy highlights in the velvety tumble of her hair.

Sebastian caught a coil of that hair between his fingertips. It was as soft and heavy as it looked. He had forgotten the pleasure of touching a woman's hair without getting powder on his hands. The steady throb of his ankle waned as a new throb shoved blood through his veins in a primal beat.

His eyes narrowed in a lazy sensuality Prudence mistook for drowsiness. "Put out the lamp," he said.

She obeyed, relieved that she had escaped being scolded or shot. Darkness drew in around them. The firelight cast flickering shadows on the far wall.

"Lie down beside me."

Her relief dissolved at the husky warmth of his voice. The darkness shrouded his features, reminding her he was a stranger, with all the dangerous edges of any unknown man met in the seductive solitude of night.

She twisted her petticoat between both hands. "I'm not very tired, thank you."

"You're not a very good liar either." His hand circled her slender wrist. "If I offend you, you may kick me in the ankle. I'm relatively harmless right now."

Prudence doubted he'd be harmless with both legs broken. No man with a mouth like that was harmless.

"I won't hurt you," he said. "Please."

It was the "please" that did it. How could she resist such good manners in a highwayman? After a moment of hesitation, she stretched out beside him, her arms and legs as rigid as boards. He slipped an arm beneath her shoulders in a casual embrace, and her head settled in the crook of his shoulder more easily than she would have hoped. Rain pattered a soothing beat on the thatched roof.

"Have you no family to worry over you?" he asked. "Won't they be frantic when you haven't returned?"

"I'm supposed to say yes, aren't I? So you'll hesitate to throttle me lest they should burst in."

He chuckled. "Perhaps you're not such a bad liar after all. Have you heard rumors of me throttling women?"

She thought for a moment. "No. But a friend of my aunt's, a Miss Devony Blake, claims you ravished her last summer. It was the talk of every picnic and ball for months. She swooned quite prettily each time she told the horrid tale."

"Which I'm sure she did," he said curtly, "in frequent and exacting detail. What do you think of this Miss Blake?"

Prudence buried her face against his collarbone. "She hasn't a brain in her silly blond head. It was more likely that she ravished you."

"So only a girl without a brain would ravish me?" His fingertips traced a teasing pattern on her arm. "Tell me—will this aunt of yours be wondering where you are?"

"She had gone to a midnight buffet when I went out. Perhaps she'll think I snuck out for an illicit tryst." Prudence smiled at the improbability of the thought.

Sebastian did not find the idea amusing. His arm tightened around her shoulders. "Did you?"

"Aye, that I did." Again, she mocked his burr with uncanny accuracy. "To meet the bonniest fellow betwixt London and Edinburgh."

Sebastian's ankle started to throb again. "Your lover?" he asked quietly.

"No, silly—my Sebastian."

Hearing his name spoken in his mistress's adoring tones, the kitten lifted his head with a drowsy purr. Sebastian took advantage of the distraction to slide his hip next to Prudence's, feeling unaccountably elated at her words. The kitten deserted the crook of his elbow and climbed onto Prudence's chest by way of her stomach.

"Fickle beast," he muttered.

He reached over to pet the animal, and his hand found the kitten's silky fur at the same moment as Prudence's. Their fingertips brushed, and she laughed breathlessly.

"It seemed such an ordinary morning when I awoke," Prudence said. "I had my bath. I put up my hair. I ate my prunes and cream." Her voice sounded odd to her, more like Devony Blake's than her own. "If anyone had told me I would be having such an extraordinary adventure by nightfall—I mean, lying in a highwayman's arms—I would have thought them insane."

He pulled his arm from beneath her and propped himself up on his elbow. "And if anyone had told you a highwayman would be kissing you?"

She swallowed. "I would have judged them a madman, lunatic, bedlamite . . ."

Her voice trailed off as his fingers entwined with her own. His head bent over her, blocking out the meager firelight, and he touched his wonderful mouth to hers. She shivered at the unfamiliar heat. He tenderly brushed his lips across hers, and with each tantalizing pass deepened the pressure, melding his lips to hers as if they had always been meant to be there. His mouth was every bit as smooth and firm as she had fancied.

"Delicious," he murmured as he pressed tiny kisses along her full bottom lip and each corner of her mouth.

No one had ever called her "delicious" before. Prudence thought she might swoon, but then he might continue to kiss her. Or worse yet, he might stop. She quenched a sharp flare of disappointment as he did just that.

His lips brushed her eyelids. "Close your eyes." His hand cupped her chin; his thumb slid sleekly across her bottom lip. "And open your mouth."

"I—I don't know," she said, her words coming in nervous spurts, "if anyone has suggested this to you before, but you have an inclination toward bossiness. It is a character flaw that might be remedied if—"

Before she could close her mouth, he swooped down and gently caught her lower lip between his teeth. Her gasp was smothered by the sly invasion of his tongue. His hand tightened on her jaw, holding her mouth open until she hadn't the will or the inclination to close it. Then his fingers slipped around to the nape of her neck in a velvety caress. His tongue swept across her teeth and delved deeper. Prudence thought she might die when she felt the shock of its warmth against her own. She should have been repulsed. Decent women did not kiss this way. But somehow having her mouth taken and stroked by this man was not repulsive, but captivating. Her own tongue responded with a tentative flick.

The highwayman groaned as if in agony, his strong fingers twisting in her hair.

She pulled back, suddenly remembering his wounded ankle. "Am I hurting you?"

"Aye, lass. You're killing me. And I love it."

In the Bestselling Tradition of Amanda Quick

LADY HELLFIRE
by Suzanne Robinson

A lush, dramatic, and touching historical romance, LADY HELLFIRE is the captivating story of a cold-blooded rogue whose dark secrets have hardened his heart to love—until he melts at the fiery touch of a sensual embrace.

After braving the perils of the wild frontier, there wasn't a man alive that Katherine Grey couldn't handle . . . or so the reckless spitfire thought . . . until she found herself on British soil, and in the presence of the devilishly disturbing Lord Alexis de Granville, Marquess of Richfield. Dangerously attractive, mysteriously tormented, he ignored her, disarmed her, enticed her. But Alexis had too many women in his life, and Kate vowed she'd never be just one more. . . .

To Alexis, women were for solace, to be used as they had always used him. Yet lovely Kate refused to play the game. One moment she scandalized him with her brash American manners, the next she seduced him with her lush lips and flame-colored hair. Worst of all, the tempestuous wench touched his faithless heart. Now, in a castle beset by treachery, Alexis will do anything, fight anyone, to make her want him as much as he needs her. . . .

Afternoon was fading when Alexis went in search of Kate again. He'd spent the intervening time trying not to think about her. He'd never tried not to think about a woman before. Never had to. It didn't work, and so he'd made the mistake of allowing himself to remember that she'd smiled upon that colossal sausage-wit Cardigan.

As soon as he did, he felt as if ants were swimming in his blood. He wanted a fight, and not just any fight, but a fight with Katherine Ann. Katie Ann. Mouthy, presumptuous, succulent Katie Ann. He found her in the kitchen garden stabbing at weeds with a trowel.

"Why are you digging in the dirt, Miss Grey?"

The blade hit a rock. Dirt flew in Kate's face and she swore.

"Hellfire. Do you have to sneak up on people and shout at them?"

Alexis studied one of his immaculate white cuffs before letting his gaze shift to the dirt on Kate's small nose. He grinned when she sputtered, discarded the trowel, and began wiping her face with the apron she wore to protect her dress.

"I asked why you are playing in my cook's garden."

"I used to take care of our garden at home. I miss it."

"Are you finished?" He held out his hand without giving her a chance to say no.

Taking Alexis's hand, she rose. "I guess I am." She placed her hands on the small of her back and leaned backward, groaning. "Oh, my. I haven't gardened in a while. What are you laughing at?"

"I don't think I've ever seen a lady pull her arms back and stick out her chest before. Not in my whole life." He laughed again at the confused look on her face and glanced pointedly at her breasts. "Your posture, Katie Ann. Gentility and maidenliness seem to be lacking across the Atlantic."

She scooped up the trowel and poked him with it. "I don't need you to tell me what maidens should or shouldn't do or talk about, Alexis de Granville. And stop grinning at me. And don't call me Katie Ann. My father is the only one who called me that."

"He must have been a brave man." He captured the hand that held the trowel. "A brave man to raise such a lightning storm of a daughter as you, Katie Ann."

He let her snatch her hand away. She rounded on him, and he watched her ire grow. She was mad enough to spit bullets. Her cheeks were flushed, her eyes bright with unladylike wrath. And he felt more alive than he had in years. Alexis couldn't help laughing again.

"You ass," she said.

"Please." He held up both hands in mock protest. "My sensibilities, Katie Ann. I shiver to think what body part you'll mention next."

"You can take all your body parts and go to hell," she said. She turned her back on him and marched across the garden to the kitchen door.

"Come back, Lady Hellfire," he called after her. "You've yet to speak of the most interesting body parts."

It was on the fourth day that she gave up all hope of understanding Alexis de Granville. She'd taken great care in selecting a hiding place in which to read. He'd found her when she'd gone to the Red Drawing Room, the Cedar Drawing Room, and the armory. This time she took refuge in the Clocktower.

The tower was a fourteenth-century construction with over fifty rooms. It stood just inside the massive barbican, the outer fortified gate house in front of the drawbridge. She selected a deserted chamber stuffed with medieval furniture and sporting a fireplace big enough for a man to stand in. What attracted her was the tall, diamond-paned window that let in the morning sunlight. The brightness streamed in and reflected off the white stone of the tower walls.

She dragged a heavy walnut chair over to the open window, then curled up in it and opened the book she'd brought with her. Her view was of the turquoise sky and a single, thin wisp of a cloud that hung like a bride's veil spread by the wind. What sounds there were came from the stirring of the pages of her book when a breeze caught them. She gradually sank into a world of bright light and beautiful words.

"Aaarrrroooof."

Kate jumped. Her knee hit the arm of her chair, and she yelped. There was a scuffling of paws, then the door to the chamber slid open under the weight of Iago's shoulder. The spaniel bounded forth. He sprang and landed with his front paws on Kate's thighs and barked again.

"Iago!" she heard Alexis call, his voice sounding too innocent.

"Damn," she said, and shoved Iago off her lap. "Go away, doggie."

Iago burrowed his head in her skirt. She got up and began pulling the dog by his collar.

"Come on, Iago. If you don't get out, he'll find me."

She was pushing on the beast from behind when the marquess stepped into the room.

"There you are, old fellow," he said. "Kate, this is a surprise."

"I don't see how. He's hunted me down three times now."

"I know. Odd, isn't it? We set out on a walk, and he comes to fetch you right away."

Iago barked, batted his paw at Alexis, and bounded out of the room.

"Now where's he going?" Kate asked. She tried not to sound annoyed.

The marquess threw up his hands in mock disgust. "I don't know. Sometimes I think he consorts with pixies so he can disappear and appear at will. What are you reading?"

Before she could stop him, he snatched the book from the chair where she'd left it.

"*Le Morte d'Arthur,*" he said. "I didn't think you'd read such romantic stuff. Knights and damsels and chivalry. Do you like romance, Miss Grey?" He didn't wait for her to answer. "Shall I read to you?"

Again he didn't wait. He started reading while leading her back to her chair. Kate frowned at him as he sank down at her feet. He was so close he almost touched her knees. She'd never had a man read to her. She was so surprised that he would want to, she let him. At first she was uncomfortable, but the sound of his voice lured her into forgetfulness. It was a low, soft voice infused with feeling and vibrancy, and it set her insides tingling in the strangest way.

The tingling made her forget the words. She listened to the sound of his voice alone. When he rested his arm on the seat of her chair, she moved so that he would have more room.

He glanced up at her and smiled. Without looking at the book, he recited. "'Then Sir Mordred sought on Queen Guinevere by letters and sounds, and by fair means and foul means, for to have her to come out of the Tower of London; but all this availed not, for she answered him shortly, openly and privily, that she had liefer slay herself than to be married with him.'"

Kate looked down at him. Inside she felt a small shiver of excitement. His voice wove a spell. It shot out magical tendrils that combined with the cool, bright air, the smell of old wood, and the warmth of his body, suffusing her in charm. She paused, balancing on an enchanted strand of faerie web between his spell and her own caution. He was looking up at her still, but his eyes changed. They became liquid metal. She started when he put his hand on hers and lifted it to his lips.

"If I were Malory," he said, "I would have Guinevere have fire-light hair and skin like the glaze on ancient porcelain. She would have earth-brown eyes and little hands that disappeared when I covered them with one of my own."

His hand slid over hers. She looked to remark that it did vanish, and when she did, he was there. His mouth came up to meet hers, and she opened her own as if it were the only thing to do.

It couldn't be helped. She wanted to kiss him, so she did.

In the bestselling tradition of Sandra Brown

WHISPERED HEAT
by Anna Eberhardt

From the moment Lissa Jamison first saw Slader Reems, she knew they belonged to each other. The tender-hearted boy sparked her youthful infatuation, but the wild and wounded young man he became lit a blazing hunger within her. Then came the night Slader was torn from her, when love was devastated by betrayal.

Holding Lissa was Slader's sweet agony on his last night of freedom. Remembering her was his sole comfort during the five years his body and soul were caged. Finally free, he's back in town to reclaim her—and everything else that was taken from him.

Slader insists Lissa belonged to him body and soul, but she knows she can't surrender to the man who could destroy her, yet who still makes her burn for his touch. She has rebuilt her life on the ashes of the past, guarding her heart in a passionless prison, and only a wildfire of longing can break her free. . . .

The jeans riding low on his hips were kept on by a whisper of a promise. He let the screen door slam, annoyed that Melissa was still sleeping, annoyed she'd disappointed him . . . *annoyed*. Lissa . . . he'd idealized her for so long, and now he had to come to terms with the real woman she'd become while he was in prison. She must really like the rich life, he thought. She hadn't stirred yet, and from the position of the sun, he'd wager it was past noon.

He opened the refrigerator and popped the cap on a beer, chugging it down to slake his thirst. What he needed next was a pair of scissors, he decided, to turn his hot jeans into a pair of cutoffs. Remembering the sewing kit that was always kept in the upstairs hall closet, he went to see if it was still there.

Reaching the upstairs hall, his gaze wandered to the master bedroom.

The door was open.

Though he tried to ignore it, he found himself drawn to it . . . the forbidden beckoning like the pages of an open diary. Without consciously willing it, he discovered himself standing in the open doorway.

The four-poster bed in the middle of the room was rumpled; the sheets were twisted. His gut twisted as well at images of Beau and Lissa there.

He heard the shower running, then saw a bathroom had been installed adjoining the bedroom, making use of the area where a small storage closet had been.

Feeling sneaky, but overwhelmed by curiosity, he ventured into the bedroom. The closet door was open. He winced when he saw Beau's clothes hanging next to Lissa's. Too intimate. It was a symbol of the reality of their marriage. He was on his way to close the door of the closet, to shut out the offending sight, when something on top of the frilly dressing table caught his eye. There, next to an open black jet-beaded box from which a string of pearls spilled, was one of the two wooden toy cars he'd made for Lissa for the Christmas that now seemed so long ago.

Both wooden cars had had wheels that worked. He rolled this one absently back and forth on the glass-covered surface. The car had changed with time; there were a few nicks and scratches, and it had darkened with age. It was incongruous next to the things on the dressing table.

Had Jamie been playing at her feet while she'd been dressing to go out one evening and left it there when she'd picked him up to put him to bed? He rather liked the idea of Lissa's son playing with the car he'd made. He thought of Jamie as Lissa's son, not Beau's.

He didn't hear the shower stop while he was lost in the world of "what ifs."

He saw her in the mirror when he looked up. She'd moved to stand beside the four-poster bed behind him. She was fluffing her hair with a pale pink towel. Obviously she didn't realize what the raising movements of her arms were doing to her breasts, so free and mobile beneath the white floor-length terry-cloth robe she had on. She'd tied the robe hastily, and it gaped just a bit to reveal a subtle flash of cleavage. She looked every inch a lady, and the slightly gaping robe gave hint she was every inch a woman.

The fragrances of soap and shampoo engulfed Slader. The herbal scent was sweet and familiar. Everything had changed in five years except the soap and shampoo she used. And his feelings.

He turned to face her.

She was still damp from her shower, as clean as he was dirty. They stood there . . . opposites.

He wanted her. He wanted her on the bed she shared with Beau. He was the one who loved her and worried about her. It should have been him, not Beau.

He walked toward her.

She didn't move.

She just stood there looking at him. Into him.

When he stopped in front of her, they were both breathing shallowly, the pupils of their eyes wide and soft. In the silence an alarm clock ticked forebodingly.

She watched a droplet of sweat slide down the stubble of his jaw and settle in the hollow of his neck. A cloud moved over the sun, throwing the room into shadow.

Slader reached out soundlessly and pulled the sash on her robe. Lissa's only reaction was an involuntary indrawn breath. The robe hung, still closed, damply molding her body. The pink towel she'd been drying her hair with slipped from her hand to the floor as she continued to stare at him.

Watching.

Waiting.

Barely breathing.

He looked into her wide soft eyes, challenging what was happening between them; his eyes showing his wonderment that she was making no move to stop it.

Her only perceptible movement was the flicker of her eyelashes as his hands reached toward her again. His forefinger rigid, he eased the robe open, his callused finger grazing the smooth swell of her left breast, leaving a dusty trail on her slick skin.

He waited.

Holding her gaze, he moved his finger to the right, his warm, dusty finger trailing the damp rise of her right breast. He pushed the robe off her shoulders, revealing her body fully to his thirsty stare.

He looked at her slowly, carefully . . . as if he were memorizing, as if he were afraid he was looking at something precious he would never be able to see again.

As she watched him his eyes gave nothing away. Not even when her nipples responded to his touch.

Melissa felt her knees weakening, desire following in the wake of the path his gaze traveled. Stepping back reflexively, she felt the edge of the bed against the back of her knees. She looked up at him expectantly.

Mesmerized, she watched as he took another step forward, pinning her against the bed without touching her. Her breath caught in her throat at the hunger in his eyes.

Her eyes drifted closed.

But Slader didn't lay her back across the bed.

When she opened her eyes, she saw that Slader had won his battle for control. He looked at her for a long moment, then turned and left the room. As quickly as it had begun, it was over.

Not one word had been exchanged between them.

FANFARE

On Sale in June

RAVISHED

☐ 29316-8 $4.99/5.99 in Canada

by Amanda Quick
<u>New York Times</u> bestselling author

Sweeping from a cozy seaside village to glittering London, this enthralling tale of a thoroughly mismatched couple poised to discover the rapture of love is Amanda Quick at her finest.

THE PRINCESS

☐ 29836-4 $5.99

by Celia Brayfield

He is His Royal Highness, the Prince Richard, and wayward son of the House of Windsor. He has known many women, but only three understand him, and only one holds the key to unlock the mysteries of his heart.

SOMETHING BLUE

☐ 29814-3 $5.99/6.99 in Canada

by Ann Hood

author of SOMEWHERE OFF THE COAST OF MAINE

"An engaging, warmly old fashioned story of the perils and endurance of romance, work, and friendship." -- <u>The Washington Post</u>

SOUTHERN NIGHTS

☐ 29815-1 $4.99/5.99 in Canada

by Sandra Chastain,
Helen Mittermeyer, and Patricia Potter

Sultry, caressing, magnolia-scented breezes. . .sudden, fierce thunderstorms. . .nights of beauty and enchantment. In three original novellas, favorite LOVESWEPT authors present the many faces of summer and unexpected love.

FANFARE

FANFARE

Rosanne Bittner

_____ 28599-8 EMBERS OF THE HEART . $4.50/5.50 in Canada
_____ 29033-9 IN THE SHADOW OF THE MOUNTAINS
$5.50/6.99 in Canada
_____ 28319-7 MONTANA WOMAN .... $4.50/5.50 in Canada
_____ 29014-2 SONG OF THE WOLF .... $4.99/5.99 in Canada

Deborah Smith

_____ 28759-1 THE BELOVED WOMAN .. $4.50/ 5.50 in Canada
_____ 29092-4 FOLLOW THE SUN .... $4.99/ 5.99 in Canada
_____ 29107-6 MIRACLE .... $4.50/ 5.50 in Canada

Tami Hoag

_____ 29053-3 MAGIC .... $3.99/4.99 in Canada

Dianne Edouard and Sandra Ware

_____ 28929-2 MORTAL SINS .... $4.99/5.99 in Canada

Kay Hooper

_____ 29256-0 THE MATCHMAKER, ... $4.50/5.50 in Canada
_____ 28953-5 STAR-CROSSED LOVERS .. $4.50/5.50 in Canada

Virginia Lynn

_____ 29257-9 CUTTER'S WOMAN, ... $4.50/4.50 in Canada
_____ 28622-6 RIVER'S DREAM, ... $3.95/4.95 in Canada

Patricia Potter

_____ 29071-1 LAWLESS .... $4.99/ 5.99 in Canada
_____ 29069-X RAINBOW .... $4.99/ 5.99 in Canada